Margaret Cevendish Duchess of Newcastle

The Cavalier and His Lady

Selections from the works of the first Duke and Duchess of Newcastle; edited with an introductory essay

Margaret Cevendish Duchess of Newcastle

The Cavalier and His Lady
Selections from the works of the first Duke and Duchess of Newcastle; edited with an introductory essay

ISBN/EAN: 9783337105983

Printed in Europe, USA, Canada, Australia, Japan

Cover: Foto ©Andreas Hilbeck / pixelio.de

More available books at **www.hansebooks.com**

THE
CAVALIER AND HIS LADY

Selections from the Works of the
First Duke and Duchess of Newcastle

EDITED WITH AN INTRODUCTORY ESSAY

BY

EDWARD JENKINS

London

MACMILLAN AND CO.

1872

THESE

CHIEFLY THE THOUGHTS

OF

A NOBLE HONOURABLE AND VIRTUOUS WOMAN

ARE

Affectionately Inscribed

TO

MY WIFE

CONTENTS.

INTRODUCTORY ESSAY

INTRODUCTORY ESSAY.

TO the visitor at Westminster Abbey, not the least striking, among its many curious monuments, will seem to be that prominent tomb in the North transept, which so quaintly perpetuates the memory and virtues of the Duke and Duchess of Newcastle. Beneath its Corinthian entablature, supported by black marble pillars, lie side by side the stony presentments of a Cavalier and his Lady: he grasps a truncheon, she a book—the latter emblem of the greatest power. And this is the legend:—

Here Lyes the Loyall Duke of Newcastle And his Dutches his second wife, by whome he had noe issue: her name was Margarett Lucas, youngest sister to the Lord Lucas of Colchester, a noble familie: for all the

Brothers were valiant, and all the Sisters virtuous. This Dutches was a wise, wittie and Learned Lady, which her many Books doe well testifie: She was a most Virtuous and a loving and careful wife and was with her Lord all the time of his banishment and miseries: and when he came home never parted from him in his solitary retirement.

A few antiquarians, bibliographers and students of history will, as they read the names, recall the romantic and changeful fortunes of the man whose effigy lies before them, or will smile at the marble book supporting the hand of the marble. Duchess, with the thought mayhap that it were as well left petrified and unsealed to after generations.

Here lies a man the vicissitudes of whose life were like the changes of an April sky, a man ennobled, through his constancy and chivalry beyond any rank of peerage, by that title of *the Loyall Duke.*

Here lies Margaret Cavendish, 'wise, wittie

and Learned, which her many Books doe well
testifie'—authoress of thirteen tomes, and more
happily not printed, friend and patroness of
not a few great men, flattered by Hobbes and
Kenelm Digby: by Ben Jonson in smooth
verses: by the Universities in rugged rhymes;
yet, I warrant, few have ever seen one of
her folios, and hardly any one ever reads
them. Many of them are rarer than gold;
while clever wit has long ago assayed them
as coin uncurrent on the 'change of literature.
Perhaps I have read them more and oftener
than any curious bookworm of these days, and
amongst sad heaps of rubbish it has seemed
to me there are a few treasures well worth the
disinterment.

Every one will remember Lamb's extravagant
praise in Elia of Her Grace's writing: 'Where
a book is at once both good and rare; where
the individual is almost the species, and when
that perishes,

> " We know not where is that Promethean torch
>   That can its light relumine."

Such a book, for instance, as the Life of the

Duke of Newcastle, by his Duchess—no casket is rich enough, no casing sufficiently durable, to honour and keep safe such a jewel.' And again,—'What moved thee, wayward, spiteful K, to be so importunate to carry off with thee in spite of tears and adjurations to thee to forbear, the Letters of that princely woman, the thrice noble Margaret Newcastle? Then, worst cut of all! to transport it with thee to the Gallican land—

> "Unworthy land to harbour such a sweetness,
> A virtue in which all ennobling thoughts dwelt,
> Pure thoughts, kind thoughts, high thoughts, her
> sex's wonder!"'

I remember when I read this I had that first-mentioned jewel lying in a dirty buff casket on my shelf, and speedily approved the prejudice of the essayist, one shared by his greater friend Coleridge. This musty tome of mine has passed through several hands, witness crest and monogram, and by one of them, nearly two centuries since, I see has been inscribed on the fly-leaf these lines from the Noble Lady's 'Poems and Fancies:'—

‘When that a Book doth from the Press come new,
All buyes or borrows it, this Book to view :
Not out of love of Learning or of Wit,
But to find faults that they may censure it.
When there’s no faults for to be found therein,
As few there are but do err in some thing,
Yet Malice with her rankled Spleen and Spight,
Will at the Time or Print or Binding bite :
Like Devills when they cannot good Soules get,
Then on the Bodies they their Witches set.’

—From the aspect of my book I judge the devils have devoted their malice to its body.

Then I resorted to Her Grace’s ‘Poems and Fancies,’ the ‘ CCXI Letters,’ ‘ The World’s Olio,’ and other works. It was often a discouraging progress : Prefaces—numerous, apologetic, remonstrative, defensive, discursive, grotesque : nine or ten of them sometimes interspersed through a volume : ‘Philosophical Opinions,’ madder than those of Alexandrian gnostic or mediæval dreamer : ‘ Tales in Prose and Verse ’ : ‘ Nature’s Pictures drawn by Phancie’s Pencil ’— a weird, rude instrument, I warrant you : plays, dialogues, orations, letters, verses on atoms, prose about atoms, allegories, more opinions, more prefaces—if there be a type of chaos or a chaos of type in literature, it is in these thirteen folios. Had I opened first on her 'philosophy,' I could scarcely have refused full credit to her own declaration:

'When I did write this book I took great pains,
For I did walk and think and break my brains.'

Nevertheless, wherever one reads in the Duchess's books, he finds the tokens of a lively, vigorous, exuberant fancy and an ingenious wit: here and there good strokes of dry, sarcastic humour: often thoughts of great force and beauty: and anon many felicitous turns of expression. There are the indisputable evidences of a genius as high-born in the realms of intellect as its possessor was exalted in the ranks of society: a genius strong-winged and swift, fertile and compre-hensive; but ruined by deficient culture, by liter-ary dissipation and the absence of two powers without which thoughts are only stray morsels of strength, I mean Concatenation and the Sense of Proportion. She thought without system and set down everything she thought. Her fancy turning round like a kaleidoscope changed its patterns and hues with the most whimsical variety and rapidity. Nevertheless I believe, had the mind of this woman been disciplined and exercised by early culture and study it would have stood out remarkable among the feminine intellects of our history. One book only, and a portion of her poem on 'Mirth and Melancholy,' have met with modern approval. The former was the 'Life of the Duke of Newcastle:' the latter was applauded in the *Connoisseur*, in a well-known paper entitled 'A vision of Female Poets.'

There exist, however, a very few copies of a brief autobiography which was attached to the first edition of 'Nature's Pictures,' but was immediately afterwards suppressed. It was entitled, 'A true Relation of my Birth, Breeding and Life: Written by the thrice Noble Illustrious and Excellent Princess, the Lady Marchioness of Newcastle,' was published in 1656, and is, in my opinion, the happiest relic of her authorship. The narrative is written with unaffected naturalness and simplicity: the character of her mother is drawn in lines so noble and pleasing as to challenge for both mother and daughter the admiration of posterity. It will in itself be the best argument for reviving Margaret Newcastle's memory after so long a trance.

She was the child of Sir Charles Lucas, whose early death left to his beautiful widow the care of several sons and daughters. Margaret was the youngest and least lively of the family, a blue stocking from childhood. She tells us in an address prefixed to the Duke's memoir, that 'it pleased God to command his servant Nature to indue me with a poetical and philosophical genius even from my birth; for I did write some books in that kind *before I was twelve years of age*, which for want of good method and order I would never divulge.' Had she been as wise at forty her editor might have had more reason to commend her. She was in 1643 sent by her own desire to the court of Queen Henrietta, but her precocious pedantry ill assorted with courtier manners. She relates very naïvely how her bashful and reticent nature, her gravity, her virtuous timidity, in a society where such graces were held in light esteem, caused her to be taken for a simpleton. She desired almost immediately to return to her home, where she could indulge her sober humours without ridicule, but her mother wisely hinted that a retirement so sudden might be injurious to the young lady's reputation, and she remained with the Queen for two years. When her Royal Mistress fled to France, Margaret Lucas attended her. In 1645, the Marquis of Newcastle roving the Continent an exile and visiting Paris, saw and chose the maid of honour for his second wife. It is said that her brother Lord Lucas had spoken of her to the Marquis with great solicitude, and it may be that his chivalry influenced his choice. They lived together very happily, mutual admirers, cherishing similar pursuits and enjoying as often as possible the quiet pleasures of country life. I must say, however, that some of the adulatory verses addressed to her by the Duke seem to be veined with the irony of which he was a master. Indeed, a doubtful story is current, that a friend once congratulating Newcastle on the wisdom of his wife, he rejoined, '*Sir, a very wise woman is a very foolish thing.*' I can hardly believe it: for the Duke was a fine-mannered gentleman and had too much respect for himself, if not for his wife, to have minted epigrams at her expense. She was of graceful person, with reserved and bashful manners, talking rarely in company. Her piety, charity and generosity were eminent. She was an economist in the household, treating her attendants with great firmness and kindness. Her excellent letter on the treatment of servants is doubtless a leaf from her own experience.

The life of the Duke is historical and he is the subject of one of Clarendon's finest portraits. The memoir written by the Duchess is brief, containing only 119 pages of what would now be a small octavo: yet the man, in the incidents of his history, the varieties of his fortunes, the habits of his private life, the strength and style of his thought, is extremely well depicted to us.

Inheriting a baronetcy at fifteen, and by

regular degrees attaining to the highest honours open to a subject, Sir William Cavendish evinced at all times considerable tact and some faculty for taking advantage of such tides of fortune as were suited to his genius and capacity. His devotion to king and state, his c ivalrous energy and self-sacrifice, his brave and able conduct in the North, brighten the pages of a melancholy history. But his intellect was not vigorous, nor did his tastes incline him to political and martial arenas. 'A very fine gentleman,' says Clarendon, 'active and full of courage, and most accomplished in those qualities of horsemanship, dancing, and fencing, which accompany a good breeding—amorous of poetry and music.' With these tastes he shrank from public affairs, was driven into them by honour against his will, and was only too glad when passion touching the same feeling in another spot, afforded him, in an insult to his pride, an excuse for abandoning them. His mind was not powerful enough, and his ambition not strong enough to impel him to persistent effort in great achievements. After brilliant feats of personal bravery or successful adventures for the royal cause, he would shut himself in with his music, and be invisible to his chief officers for two or three days at a time. No wonder Warburton styled him *a fantastical virtuoso on horseback.*

After the battle of Marston Moor, agitated with apprehensions that the Royal cause was hopelessly lost, aware that for himself there was little mercy to be expected from the rebels, and mortified by the treatment which he had experienced from Prince Rupert, he left England, with his sons and a small company of friends, for Hamburgh. Only ninety pounds remained to him of all his vast wealth, and with this, in the words of the Duchess, 'he resolved to seek his fortune.' Upon the Continent he was everywhere respectfully received and entertained, as well for the grandeur of his former estate as for his noble gallantry of demeanour. The freedom of towns was presented to him, and princes felt honoured in showing him any civility. Though often reduced to great straits his cheerful disposition kept him from despondency. The Duchess narrates that, 'After my Lord was married, having no estate or means left him to maintain himself and his family, he was necessitated to seek for credit and live upon the courtesy of those that were pleased to trust him : which although they did for some while and shewed themselves very civil to my Lord, yet they grew weary at length, insomuch that his steward was forced one time to tell him that he was not able to provide a dinner for him, for his creditors were resolved to trust him no longer. My Lord being always a great master of his passions, was—at least shewed himself—not in any manner troubled at it, but in a pleasant humour told me that I must of necessity pawn my clothes to make so much money as would procure a dinner.' The Marquis, owing to his winning manners, and 'the chief blessing of the Eternal and Merciful God who ruled the hearts of men and filled them with charity and compassion,' was able to pass his long exile in comparative comfort. Prince Charles dining with the noble pair at Antwerp, laughingly told the Duchess, ' That he perceived my Lord's credit could procure better meat than his own.'

Newcastle, who was then the first equestrian in Europe, spent much of his time in perfecting the rules of horsemanship. The exercises of the menage, which are now left to grooms and to the circus were then the manly and favourite amusement of gentlemen of quality : and the renown of his skill attracted many persons of distinction to see the Duke's performances. ' One time it happened that Don John of Austria came to Antwerp and stayed there some few days : and then almost all his court waited on my Lord, so that one day I reckoned about seventeen coaches in which were all persons of quality who came in the morning of purpose to see my Lord's menage.' He wrote a well-known treatise on horsemanship, said to be the most eminent of the kind. It is a magnificent folio adorned with illustrations of the various exercises. Several curious plates of large size and fine execution, after originals by Diepenbeke, are prefixed to the volume. One of these is worth describing.

Jupiter and the gods and goddesses are seated in the clouds watching the Marquis, who, mounted on Pegasus, is rising in the air, while eleven horses on their haunches, with forelegs and heads bent forward, offer him adoration and submission.   Beneath is this legend—

> Il monte avec la main, les éperons et gaule,
> Le cheval de Pégase qui volle en capriole;
> Il monte si haut qu'il touche de sa tête les cieux,
> Et par ses merveilles ravit en exstases les Dieux.
> Les chevaux corruptibles qui là bas sur terre sont,
> En courbettes demi-airs, terre à terre vont,
> Avec humilité soumission et bassesse,
> L'adorer comme dieu auteur de leur addresse.*

As he had foreseen the troubles of the Revolution at a time when few began to suspect the danger, so in the lowest condition of the Royal affairs he 'was never without hopes of seeing before his death a happy issue of all his misfortunes and sufferings, especially the Restoration of his most Gracious King and

---

* There is a splendid copy of this great work in the Grenville Library.   Its title is *Le Méthode Nouvelle de dresser les Cheveaux*, and it was published in 1658.   A fine edition was subsequently printed in England.

Master to his Throne and Kingly Rights.'
At the height of Cromwell's glory the Duke had
written a book in which he predicted the Restoration as an infallible certainty. He was among
the first to repair to the Hague to congratulate
the King on the recovery of his throne. The
Duchess thus relates his return to England:
' My Lord, having set sail (in an old rotten
frigate that was lost the next voyage after)
from Rotterdam, was so becalmed that he was
six days and six nights upon the water, during
which time he pleased himself with mirth and
passed his time away as well as he could;
provisions he wanted not, having them in great
store and plenty. At last being come so far
that he was able to discern the smoke of
London, which he had not seen for a long
time, he merrily was pleased to desire one that
was near him to jog and awake him out of
his dream, for surely, said he, I have been
sixteen years asleep and am not thoroughly
awake yet. My Lord lay that night at Green-
wich where his supper seemed more savoury
than any meat he had ever tasted; and the

noise of some scraping fiddlers he thought the pleasantest harmony that ever he had heard.'

Soon after the Restoration, he retired into the country and set himself to the work of repairing his estates. His houses and manors had been despoiled, his parks devastated, his woods cut down and much of his other property irretrievably destroyed. The Duchess computed his losses at £941,303, which would be an extravagant pull even on the resources of our millionnaire aristocrats in these days. But the wisdom and economy of the Duke enabled him before he died to recover in some measure his former magnificence.

Besides the huge folio on horsemanship, the Duke was the author of four plays and a number of songs, to be found scattered through his lady's publications. They afford evidences of a lively wit and some imagination, but as with her Grace, deficiency in intellectual culture and acquisition cramped the efforts of his genius. Shadwell says of him that he was the greatest master of wit, the most exact observer of mankind, and the most accurate judge of humour he ever knew. He was always a friend and patron of genius. Ben Jonson was one of his favourites, and 'fitted such scenes and speeches as he could best devise' for the rare and extravagant entertainment once prepared by Cavendish for Charles I. This *fête* is said to have cost him fourteen or fifteen thousand pounds. Hobbes was his visitor and friend, and according to the Duchess, adopted from him ideas for his 'Leviathan.' Sir William Davenant, the Poet Laureate, acted as his master of the horse ; and parson Hudson, a celebrated Divine, as his scout-master. The character of the Duke sketched by Walpole scarcely needs to be noticed. It is full of ill-nature and deficient in truth. 'Lord Clarendon,' says Brydges, 'has drawn his portrait to the life. On that rock let it stand ; without any fear that it can be shaken by the frivolous objections of Lord Orford.'

I have already touched gently upon the quality of the Duchess's mind and works. In every page there are things offensive to a fastidious or even an ordinarily healthy taste. Sometimes we are disgusted by the extreme coarseness of her images and turns of expression—a coarseness all the more remarkable because of the singular purity of her life. She had a surfeit of ideas, conceits, oddities, philosophical vagaries and poetical fancies, which she was wont to mingle in most whimsical jumbles. Like uncivilised tribes who either go natural or array themselves in grotesque habiliments, the people of her mind came forth in careless simplicity or heavy with fantastic trappings. As one of her flatterers equivocally said :

'Truth never was so naked nor so dressed.'

In the 'Vision of Female Poets' her heedlessness is amusingly satirized. 'When she came to mount, she sprang into the saddle with surprising agility; and giving an entire loose to the reins, Pegasus directly set up a gallop and ran away with her quite out of sight. However, it was acknowledged that she kept a firm seat even when the horse went at his deepest rate, and that she wanted nothing but to ride with a curb bridle.'

The vanity that here and there crops up in her writings is too simple and genuine to be offensive. It can hardly be wondered at that she should form a lofty estimate of her own poems, when she was flattered by such men as Digby, Hobbes and Bishop Pearson. There is extant a curious folio of eulogies addressed to her by several persons. Some are unique for absurd and audacious adulation. The dons of Trinity wound up a florid epistle with this compliment in the form of an epitaph:

> 'To Margaret the First:
> Princess of Philosophers:
> Who hath dispelled errors:
> Appeased the difference of opinions:
> And restored Peace
> To Learning's Commonwealth!'

A poet, in a commercial vein, asserts that had she lived in the time of the gods:

> 'She would have quite engrossed the worship trade,
> Jove and his kindred had been bankrupts made.'

This was enough to turn anyone's head.   In

an epistle to the Duke she says that when her books first came out, the world would not give her the credit of having written them : thinking 'that those conceptions and fancies transcended her capacity,' and that she had ' pluckt feathers from the Universities.' Truly 'a very preposterous judgment,' since she would never have gone well in the University curriculum. She has been termed, by literary prigs, 'the Mad Duchess,' an epithet which grates rather roughly on the feelings of one who has come into contact with her gentle thoughts. If she had a madness, it was harmless : she held it in common with many worse affected : it was authorship. She had a frenzy for creation, and was not very careful whether she produced a goldfinch or a tadpole. The temper was so inveterate, that she kept some young ladies constantly about her person to do her scribbling : and they slept near her in order that at the sound of a bell they might run to catch her wakeful fancies. She could say, with Aphrodisius in Dr. Beaumont's ' Psyche,'

' Books called me up and books put me to bed ; '

—but the books were her own. She never

studied very deeply.   As a child she wrote on
'Philosophy,' and at forty began to read books
in order to make acquaintance with its terms.
Some one at Cambridge, commencing a translation of her philosophical opinions into Latin,
gave up the task in despair.   Whether he was
captious or indolent may be judged from a
specimen selected at random : —

> 'In sinews small brain scattered lies about,
> It wants both room and quantity no doubt.
> For if a sinew could so much brain hold
> Or had a skin so large for to infold
> As in the skull : then might the toe or knee,
> Had they an optic nerve, both hear and see.
> Had sinews room fancy therein to breed,
> Copies of verses might from the heel proceed!'*

These philosophical opinions were her worst
foible: and their interspersion in her works
has hopelessly injured them for posterity.

Her Grace's poetry, which is objective in its

---

* '*Fool.*   If a man's brains were in his heels, were't not
in danger of kibes ?'.

King Lear.

character, though often extravagant and frequently spoiled by the rudeness and carelessness of the versification, is rich in image and allegory. The 'Dialogue between Mirth and Melancholy,' is usually cited as the best apology for her existence. It is not too much to say that it rivals, in their particular line, 'L'Allegro' and 'Il Penseroso,' or the well known apostrophe prefixed by Burton to the Anatomy of Melancholy. But the Duchess falls far behind the Puritan in *vif* and bell-sounding verses. Indeed neither of these melancholic poems to my judgment, comes up to the little song in the 'Nice Valour,' which is attributed to Beaumont :—

> 'Hence all you vain delights,
>   As short as are the nights
>   Wherein you spend your folly!
>   There's nought in this life sweet
>   If man were wise to see't
>   But only melancholy;
>   O sweetest melancholy!
>   Welcome folded arms and fixèd eyes,
>   A sigh that piercing mortifies,
>   A look that's fastened on the ground,
>   A tongue chained up without a sound!

Fountain heads and pathless groves,
Places which pale passion loves !
Moonlight walks where all the fowls
Are warmly housed save bats and owls !
A midnight bell, a parting groan !
These are the sounds we feed upon ;
Then stretch our bones in a still, gloomy valley ;
Nothing's so dainty sweet as lovely melancholy ?'

In the 'Pastime of the Queen of the Fairies,' we have a piece, as Brydges has said, worthy of Midsummer Night's Dream, and Milton might have envied that song of the Lady Happy as a Sea-goddess—so ethereal in its fancy, so light and melodious in its movement. The lines—

'On silver waves I sit and sing
And then the fish lie listening '—

are exquisite. She had a vivid perception of analogies which she sometimes used with great originality and effect. There are specimens of this in 'Queen Mab's Tale,' as well as in the story of 'Four Seasons of the Year.' Often her fancies are extremely delicate and ingenious, as, for instance, in the epilogue to the 'Pastime of the Fairies.'

'Sir Charles into my chamber coming in,
  When I was writing of my *Fairy Queen*;
  "I pray," said he, "when Queen Mab you do see
  Present my service to Her Majesty;
  And tell her I have heard fame's loud report
  Both of her beauty and her stately court."

'When I Queen Mab within my fancy viewed,
  My thoughts bowed low fearing I should be rude:
  Kissing her garment thin which Fancy made,
  I knelt upon a thought like one that prayed;
  And then in whispers soft I did present
  His humble service which in mirth was sent.'

There is an arch beauty in the fancy—'I knelt upon a thought.'—But as I myself prefer the pleasures of discovery to the best guidance, I will not forestal the reader's examination.

Two folios of plays written by the Duchess only serve to show how incapable she was of good dramatic writing. She had neither tenderness, passion, nor heart; therefore she could not appreciate, much less present, the finer parts of human nature, the delicate shades of sensibility, the purer and more hidden depths of feeling, or even those superb passions which the dramatic poet fills into his canvass with vivid and masterful delineation. Her cold, conversational, pedantic dialogues are to true dramatic works as a Chinese landscape is to a Cuyp or a Turner.

The little prose 'Allegories' of the Duchess, such as ' Death's Marriage,' are clever and unique. There is a picture for an artist in that wedding scene—where all the Passions and Affections, Beauty, Pleasure, Youth, Wit, Prosperity are attendants of the bride : but Health and Strength stay away; while a horrible train attends the bridegroom, for '*none that Death asked refused to come.*'   It is an old story, but limned in the few, sharp strokes of true genius.

Our authoress's Letters and Essays prove that she was a shrewd observer of minds and manners, and might have been a satirist of considerable power.   Her wit was quick and vigorous, though it dropped its shafts with unguarded carelessness. She had not even the industry to chisel and polish the figures her genius had invented. Nevertheless its power is evident in numberless instances. Some of her aphorisms are Baconian.   For example : ' Wine, though it begins like a friend, goes on like a fool, and most commonly ends like a devil in a fury.' Or again : 'Most men's minds are insipid, having no balsamical virtue therein : they are as the *terra damnata* of nature.' The 'Essay on Fools' is an admirable satire. 'The captious fool is as a troubled water where no beast can drink.' One ,is startled with the tremendous and concentrated force of an epigram like this. I particularly like the wisdom of that essay on 'Gentlewomen that are sent to Boarding Schools.'

The Duchess abstained on principle from correcting or revising her books, 'lest it should disturb her following conceptions !' Hence the patience of one who reads the original publications is extremely racked by a multitude of patent errors, ambiguities and solecisms, while his taste is shocked by clumsy sentences, bad rhymes and rugged verses. I take the liberty in preparing these selections for modern eyes and tastes, to perform for the Duchess the task she should have undertaken for herself. Where, without very serious alterations, I could see my way to correct obvious errors, or improve the text, I have done so, though everywhere with a hesitat-

ing and careful hand. To me it seems a foolish
and inutile affectation to reproduce with too
ingenious care the blunders of old authors and
the monstrosities of their printers. The alterations I have ventured upon are few enough to
be of no great consequence. Subject to this
explanation the reader may find in these pages
far more than has justified many modern re-
productions of obsolete authors.

When we search the trunk of oblivion for the
muniments of genius we too often find them to
afford only delusive evidences of rightful claims,
or that the force of them has been cancelled by
the lapse of time. Seldom do we, as in the
case of the Cavalier and his Lady, fall in with
parchments which are deeds of honest genius,
still conveying to posterity some worthy in-
heritance.

E. J.

A TRUE RELATION

OF

MY BIRTH, BREEDING AND LIFE:

WRITTEN

BY THE THRICE

NOBLE, ILLUSTRIOUS AND EXCELLENT

PRINCESS, THE

LADY MARCHIONESS OF NEWCASTLE.

1656.

A true Relation, &c.

Y father was a gentleman; which title is given and grounded by merit, not by princes; and 'tis the act of time not favour. And though my father was not a peer of the realm, yet there were few peers who had much greater estates or lived more noble therewith. Yet at that time great titles were to be sold, and not at so high rates but that his estate might have easily purchased one, and he was prest for to take; but my father did not esteem titles unless they were gained by heroick actions, and the kingdom being in a happy peace with all other nations, and in itself being governed by a wise king, King *James*, there were no employments for heroick spirits. Towards the latter end of Queen *Elizabeth's* reign, as soon as he came to man's estate, he unfortunately fortunately killed one Mr. *Brooks* in a single duel.

For my father by the laws of honour could do no less than call him to the field to question him for an injury he did him: where their swords were to dispute and one or both of their lives to decide the argument, wherein my father had the better: and though my father by honour challenged him, with valour fought him, and in justice killed him, yet he suffered more than any person of quality usually doth in cases of honour; for though the laws be rigorous, yet the present princes most commonly are gracious in those misfortunes, especially to the injured. But my father found it not, for his exile was from the time of his misfortunes to Queen *Elizabeth's* death. For the Lord *Cobham*, being then a great man with Queen *Elizabeth*, and this gentleman Mr. *Brooks* a kind of a favourite and as I take it brother to the then Lord Cobham, made Queen *Elizabeth* so severe as not to pardon him. But King *James* of blessed memory, graciously gave him his pardon and leave to return home to his native country, wherein he lived happily and died peaceably, leaving a wife and eight children, three sons and five daughters,

I being the youngest child he had, and an infant when he died.

As for my breeding, it was according to my birth and the nature of my sex: for my birth was not lost in my breeding. For as my sisters were or had been bred so was I bred, in plenty —or rather with superfluity. Likewise we were bred virtuously, modestly, civilly, honourably, and on honest principles. As for plenty, we had not only for necessity, conveniency and decency, but for delight and pleasure to superfluity. We did not riot, but we lived orderly; for riot, even in kings' courts and princes' palaces, brings ruin without content or pleasure: while order, in less fortunes, shall live more plentifully and deliciously than princes that live in a hurly-burly, as I may term it, in which they are seldom well-served. For disorder obstructs: besides, it doth disgust life, distract the appetites, and yield no true relish to the senses. For Pleasure, Delight, Peace and Felicity live in method and temperance.

As for our garments, my Mother did not only delight to see us neat and cleanly, fine and gay, but rich and costly: maintaining us to the heighth of her estate, but not beyond it. For we were so far from being in debt before these wars, as we were rather beforehand with the world : buying all with ready money, not on the score. For although after my father's death the estate was divided between my Mother and her sons, paying such a sum of money for portions to her daughters either at the day of their marriage or when they should come to age, yet by reason she and her children agreed with a mutual consent, all their affairs were managed so well, as she lived not in a much lower condition than when my father lived. 'Tis true my Mother might have increased her daughters' portions by a thrifty sparing : yet she chose to bestow it on our breeding, honest pleasures and harmless delights : out of an opinion that if she bred us with needy necessity it might chance to create in us sharking qualities, mean thoughts, and base actions, which she knew my Father as well as herself did abhor. Likewise we were bred tenderly, for my Mother naturally did strive to please and delight her children, not to cross or torment them, terrifying them with threats or lashing them with slavish whips; but, instead of threats, reason was used to persuade us; and instead of lashes, the deformities of vice were discovered: and the graces and virtues were presented unto us. Also we were bred with respectful attendance, every one being severally waited upon: and all her servants in general used the same respect to her children (even those that were very young) as they did to herself; for she suffered not her servants either to be rude before us or to domineer over us, which all vulgar servants are apt, and oftimes have leave to do. She never suffered the vulgar serving-men to be in the nursery among the nurse maids, lest their rude love-making might do unseemly actions or speak unhandsome words in the presence of her children; knowing that youth is apt to take infection by ill examples, having not the reason to distinguish good from bad. Neither were we suffered to have any familiarity or conversation with the vulgar servants: yet she caused us to demean ourselves with an humble civility towards them, as they with a dutiful respect to us. Not because they were servants were we so reserved, for many noble persons are forced to serve through necessity, but by reason the vulgar sort of servants are as ill bred as meanly born, giving children ill examples and worse counsel.

As for tutors, although we had all sorts of virtuosos *, as for singing, dancing, playing on music, reading, writing, working and the like, yet we were not kept strictly thereto : they were rather for formality than benefit : for my Mother cared not so much for our dancing and fiddling, singing and prating of several languages; as that we should be bred virtuously, modestly, civilly, honourably and in honest principles.

As for my brothers, of whom I had three, I know not how they were bred. First, they

---

* Originally this was printed 'although for all sorts of *virtues*;' but in the copy attached to 'Tales in Prose and Verse,' in the King's Library at the British Museum, the Duchess has with her own hand altered virtues into 'virtuosos.' I have arranged the text accordingly.

were bred when I was not capable to observe or before I was born : likewise the breeding of men is of a different manner from that of women. But this I know, that they loved virtue, endeavoured merit, practised justice and spoke truth : they were constantly loyal and truly valiant. Two of my brothers were excellent soldiers and martial discipliners, being practised therein. For though they might have lived upon their own estates very honourably, yet they rather chose to serve in the wars under the States of Holland, than to live idly at home in peace ; my brother Sir *Thomas Lucas* there having a troop of horse, my brother the youngest Sir *Charles Lucas* serving therein. But he served the States not long, for after he had been at the siege and taking of some towns, he returned home again. And though he had the less experience yet he was like to have proved the better soldier, if better could have been, having naturally a practick genius to the warlike arts, as natural poets have to poetry. But his life was cut off before he could arrive to the perfection thereof. Yet he writ a treatise of the Arts in War; but by reason it was in characters and the key thereof lost, we cannot as yet understand anything therein, at least not so as to divulge it. My other brother, the Lord *Lucas*, who was heir to my father's estate, and as it were the father to take care of us all, is not less valiant than they were, although his skill in the discipline of war was not so much, not being bred therein. Yet he had more skill in the use of the sword, and is more learned in other arts and sciences than they were: he being a great scholar by reason he is given much to studious contemplation.

Their practice was when they met together, to exercise themselves with fencing, wrestling, shooting, and such like exercises: for I observed they did seldom hawk or hunt and very seldom or never dance or play on music, saying it was too effeminate for masculine spirits. Neither had they skill or did use to play for aught I could hear, at cards or dice or the like games: nor [were they] given to any vice, as I did know, unless to love a mistress were a crime. Not that I know they had any but what report did say, and usually reports are false—at least exceed the truth.

As for the pastimes of my sisters when they were in the country, it was to read, work, walk and discourse with each other. For though two of my three brothers were married, my brother, the Lord Lucas, to a virtuous and beautiful lady, daughter to Sir *Christopher Neville*, son to the *Lord Abergaveny;* and my brother, Sir *Thomas Lucas*, to a virtuous lady of an ancient family, one Sir *John Byron's* * daughter; likewise three of my four sisters, one married Sir *Peter Killigrew*, the other Sir *William Walter*, the third Sir *Edmund Pye*, the fourth as yet unmarried; yet most of them lived with my Mother, especially when she was at her country house: living most commonly at *London* half the year, which is the metropolitan city of England. But when they were at *London* they were dispersed into several houses of their own: yet for the most part they met every day, feasting each other like

---

* Sister to the ancestor of Lord Byron.—*Brydges*.

Job's children. But this unnatural war came like a whirlwind which fell'd down their houses; where some in the wars were crushed to death—as my youngest brother Sir *Charles Lucas* and my brother Sir *Thomas Lucas*. And though my brother Sir *Thomas Lucas* died not immediately of his wounds, yet a wound he received on his head in *Ireland* shortened his life.

But to rehearse their recreations. Their custom was in winter-time to go sometimes to plays or to ride in their coaches about the streets to see the concourse and recourse of people. And in the spring-time to visit the Spring-garden, Hyde Park and the like places. And sometimes they would have music and sup in barges upon the water. These harmless recreations they would pass their time away with. For I observed they did seldom make visits, nor never went abroad with strangers in their company, but only themselves in a flock together, agreeing so well that there seemed but one mind amongst them. And not only my own brothers and sisters agreed so but my brothers and sisters in law; and their children, although but young, had the like agreeable natures and affectionate dispositions. For to my best remembrance I do not know that ever they did fall out or had any angry or unkind disputes. Likewise I did observe that my sisters were so far from mingling themselves with any other company, that they had no familiar conversation or intimate acquaintance with the families to which each other were linked by marriage, the family of the one being as great strangers to the rest of my brothers and sisters as the family of the other.

But sometime after this war began I knew not how they lived. For though most of them were in *Oxford* where the king was, yet after the Queen went from *Oxford* and so out of *England*, I was parted from them. When the Queen was at *Oxford*, I had a great desire to be one of her maids-of-honour, hearing the Queen had not the same number she was used to have. Whereupon I wooed and won my Mother to let me go, for my Mother being fond of all her children was desirous to please them, which made her consent to my request. But my brothers and sisters seemed not very well pleased by reason I had never been from home nor seldom out of their sight: for though they knew I would not behave myself to their or my own dishonour, yet they thought I might to my disadvantage, being unexperienced in the world. Which indeed I did; for I was so bashful when I was out of my Mother's, brothers' and sisters' sight, whose presence used to give me confidence—thinking I could not do amiss whilst any one of them were by, for I knew they would gently reform me if I did: besides, I was ambitious they should approve of my actions and behaviour—that when I was gone from them I was like one that had no foundation to stand or guide to direct me, which made me afraid lest I should wander with ignorance out of the ways of honour. So that I knew not how to behave myself. Besides I had heard the World was apt to lay aspersions even on the innocent, for which I durst neither look up with my eyes, nor speak, nor be any way sociable, insomuch as I was thought a natural fool. Indeed I had not much wit, yet I was not an idiot—my wit was according to my years. And though I might have learnt more wit and advanced my understanding by living in a Court, yet being dull, fearful and bashful, I neither heeded what was said or practised, but just what belonged to my loyal duty and my own honest reputation. Indeed, I was so afraid to dishonour my friends and family by my indiscreet actions, that I rather chose to be accounted a fool, than to be thought rude or wanton. In truth my bashfulness and fears made me repent my going from home to see the world, and much did I desire to return to my mother again, or to my sister *Pye*, with whom I often lived when she was in *London* and loved with a supernatural affection. But my Mother advised me then to stay, although I put her to more charges than if she had kept me at home, and she maintained me so that I was in a condition rather to lend than to borrow; which courtiers usually are not. But my Mother said it would be a disgrace for me to return out of the Court so soon after I was placed. So I continued almost two years, until such time as I was married thence: for my Lord the Marquis of *Newcastle* did approve of those bashful fears which many condemned, and would choose such a wife as he might bring to his own humours and not such an one as was wedded to self-conceit, or one that had been tempered to the humours of another—for which he wooed me for his wife. And though I did dread marriage and shunned men's companies as much as I could, yet I could not nor had not the power to refuse him, by reason my affections were fixed on him: and he was the only person I ever was in love with. Neither was I ashamed to own it but gloried therein. For it was not amorous love. I never was infected therewith. It is a disease, or a passion, or both—I only know by relation, not by experience. Neither could title, wealth, power or person entice me to love; but my love was honest and honourable being placed upon merit. Which affection joyed at the fame of his worth, was pleased with delight in his wit, was proud of the respect he used to me, and triumphed in the affections he professed for me. Those affections he hath confirmed to me by a deed of time, sealed by constancy and assigned by an unalterable decree of his promise, which makes me happy in despite of Fortune's frowns. For though Misfortunes may and do oft dissolve base, wild, loose and ungrounded affections, yet they have no power over those that are united either by merit, justice, gratitude, duty, fidelity or the like. And though my Lord hath lost his estate and been banished out of his country for his loyalty to his King and country, yet neither despised poverty nor pinching necessity could make him break the bonds of friendship or weaken his loyal duty.

But not only the family I am linked to is ruined, but the family from which I sprung by these unhappy wars. Which ruin my Mother lived to see and then died, having lived a widow for many years: for she never forgot my Father so as to marry again. Indeed he remained so lively in her memory and her

grief was so lasting as she never mentioned
his name (though she spoke often of him)
but love and grief caused tears to flow, and
tender sighs to rise—mourning in sad complaints. She made her house her cloister,
inclosing herself, as it were, therein : for she
seldom went abroad unless to church. But
these unhappy wars forced her out, by reason
she and her children were loyal to the King;
for which they plundered her and them of all
their goods, plate, jewels, money, corn, cattle
and the like—cut down their woods, pulled
down their houses, and sequestered them from
their lands and livings. In such misfortunes
my Mother was of an heroic spirit, in suffering
patiently when there was no remedy, and being
industrious where she thought she could help.
She was of a grave behaviour and had such
a majestic grandeur as it were continually
hung about her, that it would strike a kind of
awe into the beholders and command respect
from the rudest—(I mean the rudest of civilized
people—I mean not such barbarous people
as plundered her and used her cruelly—for

they would have pulled God out of Heaven, had they had power, as they did Royalty out of his throne). Her beauty was beyond the ruin of time, for she had a well-favoured loveliness in her face, a pleasing sweetness in her countenance, and a well tempered complexion, neither too red nor too pale, even to her dying hour, although in years. And by her dying one might think Death was enamoured of her, for he embraced her in a sleep and so gently as if he were afraid to hurt her. She was an affectionate Mother, breeding her children with a most industrious care and tender love. Having eight children, there was not any one crooked or any ways deformed, neither were they dwarfish or of giantlike stature, but every way proportionable, well-featured, [with] clear complexions, brown hairs, sound teeth, sweet breath, plain speeches, tunable voices—I mean not so much to sing, as in speaking—as not stuttering, nor wharling in the throat or speaking through the nose or hoarsely, or squeakingly, which impediments many have : neither were their voices of

too low a strain or too high, but their notes
and words were tunable and timely.

I hope this truth will not offend my readers;
and lest they should think I am a partial
register, I dare not commend my sisters, as to
say they were handsome, although many would
say they were very handsome. But this I dare
say: their beauty, if they had any, was not so
lasting as my mother's, time making suddener
ruin in their faces than in hers.

My Mother was a good mistress to her servants, taking care of them in their sicknesses,
not sparing any cost she was able to bestow for
their recovery. Neither did she exact from them
more in their health than what they with ease,
or rather like pastime, could do. She would
freely pardon a fault, and forget an injury—
yet sometimes she would be angry: but never
with her children, for the sight of them would
pacify her. Neither would she be angry with
others but when she had cause—as with negli-
gent or knavish servants, that would lavishly
or unnecessarily waste or subtilly and thievishly.
steal. And, though she would often complain

that her family was too great for her weak management and often prest my brother to take it upon him, yet I observed, she took a pleasure and some little pride in the governing thereof. She was very skilful in leases, and setting * of lands, and Court-keeping, ordering of stewards† and the like affairs. Also I observed that my Mother, or brother before these wars, had never any lawsuits but what an attorney despatched in a term with small cost. If they had it was more than I knew of. But, as I said, my mother lived to see the ruin of her children in which was her ruin — and then died. My brother Sir *Thomas Lucas* died soon after, my brother Sir *Charles Lucas* after him, being shot to death for his loyal service; for he was most constantly loyal and courageously active, indeed he had a superfluity of courage. My eldest sister died some time before my mother, her death being as I believe hastened through grief of her only daughter on whom she doted, being very pretty,

---

* I. e. letting ; or perhaps allotting
† The Courts and stewards of the manors.

sweet-natured, and having an extraordinary wit for her age. She dying of a consumption, my sister her mother died some half a year after of the same disease: and though Time is apt to waste remembrance as a consumptive body or to wear it out like a garment into rags, or to moulder it into dust, yet I find the natural affections I have for my friends are beyond the length, strength and power of Time, for I shall lament the loss so long as I live. So also shall I lament the loss of my Lord's Noble Brother who died not long after I returned from *England* he being then sick of an ague: whose favours and my thankfulness, ingratitude shall never disjoin. For I will build his monument of truth, though I cannot of marble, and hang my tears as scutcheons on his tomb. He was nobly generous, wisely valiant, naturally civil, honestly kind, truly loving, virtuously temperate: his promise was like a fixt decree, his words were destiny; his life was holy, his disposition mild, his behaviour courteous, his discourse pleasing; he had a ready wit and a spacious knowledge, a settled judgment, a clear understanding, a rational insight; he was learned in all arts and sciences, but especially in the mathematics in which study he spent most part of his time: and though his tongue preached not moral philosophy yet his life taught it: indeed he was such a person that he might have been a pattern for all mankind to take. He loved my Lord his brother with a doting affection as my Lord did him; for whose sake I suppose he was so nobly generous, carefully kind and respectful to me; for I dare not challenge his favours as to myself, having not merits to deserve them. He was for a time the preserver of my life. For after I was married some two or three years my Lord travelled out of France, from the city of *Paris*, in which city he resided the time he was in *France*, into *Holland*, to *Rotterdam*: where he stayed some six months. From thence he returned to *Brabant*, unto the city of *Antwerp*, which city we had passed through when we went into *Holland*, and in that city, my Lord settled himself and family, choosing it for the pleasantest and quietest place to retire himself and his ruined fortunes in. But after we had remained sometime therein, we grew extremely necessitated, tradesmen being there not so rich, as to trust my Lord for so much or so long as those in France. Yet they were so civil, kind and charitable as to trust him for as much as they were able. But at last necessity enforced me to return into England to seek for relief. For I, hearing my Lord's estate amongst many more estates was to be sold, and that the wives of the owners should have an allowance therefrom, it gave me hopes I should receive a benefit thereby. So being accompanied by my Lord's only brother, Sir *Charles Cavendish*, who was commanded to return, to live therein or to lose his estate — over I went. But when I came there I found their hearts as hard as my fortunes, and their natures as cruel as my miseries: for they sold all my Lord's estate which was a very great one and gave me not any part thereof, or any allowance thereout, so that few or no other was so hardly dealt withal. Indeed I did not stand as a beggar at the Parliament door, for I never was at the Parliament-House, nor stood I ever at the door as I do know or can remember; not as a petitioner I am sure. Neither did I haunt the Committees, for I never was at any as a petitioner, but one in my life, which was at Goldsmith's Hall, but I received neither gold nor silver from them, only an absolute refusal that I should have any of my Lord's estate. My brother, Lord *Lucas* did claim in my behalf such a part of my Lord's estate as wives had allowed them, but they told him that by reason I was married since my Lord was made a delinquent I could have nothing nor should have anything he being the greatest traitor to the State—which was to be the most loyal subject to his King and Country. But I whisperingly spoke to my brother to conduct me out of that ungentlemanly place, so without speaking unto them one word good or bad I returned to my lodgings, and as that Committee was the first, so was it the last I ever was at as a petitioner. 'Tis true I went sometimes to Drury House to inquire how the land was sold: but no other ways, although some reported I was at the Parliament-House, and at this Committee and that Committee, and what I said and how I was answered. But the customs of England are changed as well as the laws, where women become pleaders, attorneys, petitioners and the like, running about with their several causes, complaining of their several grievances, exclaiming against their several enemies, bragging of their several favours they receive from the powerful; thus trafficking with idle words brings in false reports and vain discourse. For the truth is our sex doth nothing but jostle for the preeminence of words (I mean not for speaking well but speaking much) as they do for the preeminence of place, words rushing against words, thwarting and crossing each other, pulling with reproaches, striving to throw each other down with disgrace, thinking to advance themselves thereby. But if our sex would but well consider and rationally ponder, they will perceive and find that it is neither words nor place that can advance them, but worth and merit. Nor can words or place disgrace them, but inconstancy and boldness:

for an honest heart, a noble soul, a chaste life and a true-speaking tongue is the throne, sceptre, crown and footstool that advances them to an honourable renown. . . . But I despairing because I was positively denied at Goldsmith's Hall (besides I had a firm faith or strong opinion that the pains was more than the gains), and being unpractised in public employments, unlearned in their uncouth ways; ignorant of the humours and dispositions of those persons to whom I was to address my suit, and not knowing where the power lay and not being a good flatterer, did not trouble myself to petition my enemies. Besides I am naturally bashful. Not that I am ashamed of my mind or body, my birth or breeding, my actions or fortunes, for my bashfulness is in my nature, not for any crime. And though I have striven and reasoned with myself, yet that which is inbred I find it difficult to root out. I do not find that my bashfulness is concerned with the qualities of the persons, but the number; for were I to enter into a company of *Lazaruses* I should be as much out of countenance as

if they were all *Cesars*, or *Alexanders*, *Cleo-
patras* or *Queen Didos*. Neither do I find my
bashfulness riseth so often in blushes as it con-
tracts my spirits to a chill paleness. But the
best of it is, most commonly it soon vanisheth
away and many times before it can be perceived:
and the more foolish or unworthy I conceive
the company to be the worse I am, and the
best remedy I ever found is to persuade myself
that all those persons I meet are wise and
virtuous. The reason I take to be this: that
the wise and virtuous censure least, excuse
most, praise best, esteem rightly, judge justly,
behave themselves civilly, demean themselves
respectfully and speak modestly, when fools or
unworthy persons are apt to commit absurdities,
and be bold, rude, uncivil both in words and
actions, forgetting or not well understanding
themselves or the company they are with.
And though I never met such sorts of ill-bred
creatures, yet naturally I have such an aversion
to them, as that I am afraid to meet them,
as children are afraid of spirits or others are
afraid to see or meet devils: which makes me

think this natural defect in me, if it be a defect, is rather a fear than a bashfulness. But whatsoever it is I find it troublesome, for it hath many times obstructed the passage of my speech and perturbed natural actions, forcing a constrainedness or unusual motions. However since it is rather a fear of others than a bashful distrust of myself I despair of a perfect cure, unless Nature as well as human governments should be civilized and brought into a methodical order, ruling words and actions with a supreme power of Reason and the authority of discretion. A rude nature is worse than a brute nature by so much more as man is better than a beast: and those that are of civil natures and genteel dispositions are as much nearer to celestial creatures as those that are rude and cruel are to devils.

In fine, after I had been in England a year and a half, in which time I gave some half a score visits and went with my Lord's brother to hear music in one Mr. *Lawes's* * house,

---

* Lawes was a celebrated musical composer, the friend of Milton.—*Brydges.*

three or four times, as also some three or
four times to *Hyde Park* with my sisters, to
take the air, else I never stirred out of my
lodgings unless to see my brothers and sisters,
and seldom did dress myself, taking no delight
to adorn myself, since he I only desired to
please was absent, although report did dress
me in a hundred several fashions. In part of
the time I wrote a book of Poems and a
little book called my *Philosophical Fancies*, to
which I have written a large addition since I
returned out of England, besides this book and
one other. As for my book entitled *The
World's Olio*, I wrote most part of it before I
went into England. But being not of a merry,
although not of a froward or peevish disposition, I became very melancholy by reason I
was from my Lord, which made my mind so
restless that it did break my sleep and distemper
my health ; with which, growing impatient of a
longer delay, I resolved to return, although I
was grieved to leave Sir *Charles*, he being
sick of an ague : of which sickness he died :
for though his ague was cured his life was

decayed, for the dregs of his ague did put out the lamp of his life. . . . . Yet Heaven knows I did not think his life was so near an end, for his doctor had great hopes of his perfect recovery. So I made haste to return to my Lord, with whom I had rather be as a poor beggar than to be mistress of the world absented from him. Heaven hitherto hath kept us, and though Fortune hath been cross yet we do submit and are both content with what is and cannot be mended, and are so prepared, that the worst of fortunes shall not afflict our minds so as to make us unhappy, howsoever it doth pinch our lives with poverty. For, if tranquillity lives in an honest mind the mind dwells in peace, although the body suffer. But Patience hath armed us and Misery hath tried us and find us Fortune-proof. For the truth is my Lord, is a person whose humour is neither extravagantly merry nor unnecessarily sad; his mind is above his fortune, as his generosity is above his purse, his courage above danger, his justice above bribes, his friendship above self-interest, his truth too firm for falsehood, his temperance beyond temptation. His conversation is pleasing and affable, his wit is quick and his judgment strong, distinguishing clearly without clouds of mistakes, dissecting truths so as they justly admit not of disputes: his discourse is always new upon the occasion without troubling the hearers with old historical relations, nor stuffed with useless sentences. His behaviour is manly without formality and free without constraint : and his mind hath the same freedom. His nature is noble, and his disposition sweet. His loyalty is proved by his public service for his King and Country, by his often hazarding of his life, by the loss of his estate and the banishment of his person, by his necessitated condition and his constant and patient suffering. But howsoever our fortunes are we are both content, spending our time harmlessly; for my Lord pleaseth himself with the management of some few horses and exercises himself with the use of the sword; which two arts he hath brought by his studious thoughts, rational experience and industrious practice to an absolute perfection. And though he hath taken as much pains in those arts both by study and practice as chemists for the philosopher's stone, yet he hath this advantage of them, that he hath found the right and truth thereof and therein ; which chemists never found in that pursuit and never will. He also recreates himself with his pen, writing what his wit dictates to him. But I pass my time rather with scribbling than writing, with words than wit. Not that I speak much because I am addicted to contemplation unless I am with my Lord, yet then I rather attentively listen to what he says than impertinently speak. When I am writing any sad feigned stories or serious humours or melancholy passions, I am forced many times to express them with the tongue before I can write them with the pen, by reason those thoughts that are sad, serious and melancholy are apt to contract and to draw too much back, which oppression doth as it were over-power or smother the conception in the brain. But when some of those thoughts are sent out in words they give the rest more liberty to place themselves in a more methodical order, marching more regularly with my pen on the ground of white paper. But my letters seem rather as a ragged rout than a well-armed body, for the brain being quicker in creating than the hand in writing or the memory in retaining, many fancies are lost, by reason they oft-times outrun the pen, while I, to keep speed in the race, write so fast as I stay not so long as to write my letters plain, insomuch as some have taken my hand-writing for some strange character. . . . . . However, that little wit I have it delights me to scribble it out and disperse it about. For I being addicted from my childhood to contemplation rather than conversation, to solitariness rather than society, to melancholy rather than mirth, to write with the pen rather than to work with a needle; passing my times with harmless fancies, their company being pleasing, their conversation innocent,—I take such pleasure therein as to neglect my health : for it is as great a grief to leave their society as a joy to be in their company. My only trouble is lest my brain should grow barren, or that the root of my fancies should become insipid, withering into a dull stupidity for want of maturing subjects to write on ;* for I am of a lazy nature and not of an active disposition as some are that love to journey from town to town, from house to house, delighting in variety of company, making one where the greatest number is. In playing cards or any other games I neither have practised nor have I any skill therein. As for dancing, although it be a graceful art and becometh unmarried persons well, yet for those that are married it is too light an action, disagreeing with the gravity of that state. For revelling I am of too dull a nature to make one of a merry society : as for feasting it would neither agree with my humour nor constitution, for my diet is for the most part sparing—as a little boiled chicken or the like and my drink most commonly water. For though I have an indifferent good appetite, yet

---

* The Duchess could not more happily have expressed her intellectual fate.

I do often fast, out of an opinion that if I should eat much and exercise little (which I do, only walking a slow pace in my chamber whilst my thoughts run apace in my brain, so that the motions of my mind hinder the active exercises of the body) I should soon injure myself. Should I dance or run or walk apace I should dance my thoughts out of measure, run my fancies out of breath and tread out the feet of my numbers. But because I would not bury myself quite from the sight of the world I go sometimes abroad, seldom to visit but only in my coach about the town,* which we call here a *tour*, where all the chief of the town go to see and be seen, likewise all strangers of what quality soever, as all great princes or queens that make any stay : for this town being a passage or thoroughfare to most parts, causeth many times persons of great quality to be here, though not as inhabitants, yet to lodge for some short time, and all such as I said, take delight, or at least go, to see

---

* Antwerp, where this was written.

the custom thereof. Most cities of note in Europe for all I can hear, have such like re-creations for the effeminate sex. Although for my part I had rather sit at home and write: but I hold it necessary sometimes to appear abroad: besides I find that several objects bring new materials for my thoughts and fancies to build upon. Yet I must say this in behalf of my thoughts, that I never found them idle: for if the senses bring no work in, they will work of themselves, like silk worms that spin out of their own bowels. Neither can I say I think the time tedious when I am alone, so long as I be near my Lord and know he is well.

Now I have declared to my readers my Birth, Breeding and Actions to this time of my life. I mean the material parts thereof, for should I write every particular, as my childish sports and the like, it would be ridiculous and tedious. I have been honour-ably born and nobly matched: I have been bred to elevated thoughts not to a de-jected spirit: my life hath been ruled with honesty, attended by modesty, and directed by truth.*

Since I have written in general thus far of my life, I think it fit I should speak something of my humour, particular practice and disposition. As for my humour I was from my childhood given to contemplation, being more taken and delighted with thoughts than in conversation with a society, insomuch, as I would walk two or three hours, and never rest, in a musing, considering, contemplating manner, reasoning with myself of everything my senses did present ; but when I was in the company of my natural friends I was very attentive of what they said and did. For strangers I regarded not much what they said but I observed their actions, whereupon my reason as judge, my thoughts as accusers or excusers or approvers and commenders did plead or appeal or complain thereto.

---

* O rare, illustrious Princess! How many of thy sex could then or now have written of themselves the like in every particular ?

Also I never took delight in closets or cabinets of toys, but in the variety of fine clothes and such toys only as were to adorn my person. Likewise I had a natural stupidity towards the learning of any other language than my native tongue; for I could sooner and with more facility understand the sense, than remember the words, and the want of such memory makes me so unlearned in foreign languages as I am.

As for my practice,* I was never very active by reason I was given so much to contemplation; besides, my brothers and sisters were for the most part serious and staid in their actions, not given to sport or play, or dancing about, whose company, I keeping, became so too. But I observed although their actions were staid, yet they would be very merry amongst themselves, delighting in each other's company. Also they would in their discourse express the general actions of the world: judging, con-

---

* Used here in the sense of habits of life—though correctly habits are the result of practice or use. Further on she more properly uses the word in another sense, namely, in that of an employment.

demning, approving, commending as they thought good, and with those that were innocently harmless they would make themselves merry.

As for my study of books it was little, yet I chose rather to read than to employ my time in any other work or practice. But my serious study could not be much by reason I took great delight in attiring, fine dressing and fashions, especially such fashions as I did invent myself, not taking that pleasure in such fashions as were invented by others. I did dislike that any should follow my fashions, for I always took delight in a singularity, even in accoutrements of habits. But whatsoever I was addicted to either in fashions of clothes, contemplation of thought, actions of life — they were lawful, honest, honourable and modest, which I can avouch to the world with a great confidence because it is a pure truth. As for my disposition it is more inclining to melancholy than merry, but not crabbed or peevish melancholy, but soft, melting solitary and contemplative melancholy. And I am apt to weep rather than laugh, not that I often do either of them. Also I am tender-natured, for it troubles my conscience to kill a fly and the groans of a dying beast strike my soul. Also where I place a particular affection, I love extraordinarily and constantly, yet not fondly but soberly and observingly: not to hang about them [I love] as a trouble, but to wait upon them as a servant. This affection will take no root but where I think or find merit, and have leave both from Divine and moral laws. Yet I find this passion so troublesome, that it is the only torment of my life; for fear any evil misfortune, or accident, or sickness or death should come unto them—insomuch that I am never freely at rest. Likewise I am grateful: for I never receive a courtesy but I am impatient and troubled until I can return it. Also I am chaste both by nature and education insomuch as I do abhor an unchaste thought. Likewise I am seldom angry as my servants may witness for me, for I rather choose to suffer some inconveniences than disturb my thoughts, which makes me many times wink at their faults: but when I am angry

I am very angry—but yet it is soon over and I am easily pacified if it be not such an injury as to create a hate. Neither am I apt to be exceptious or jealous, but if I have the least symptom of that passion, I declare it to those it concerns, for I never let it lie smouldering in my breast to breed a malignant disease in the mind, which might break out in extravagant passions, or railing speeches, or indiscreet actions. But I examine moderately, reason soberly, and plead gently in my own behalf; through a desire to keep those affections I had, or at least thought to have. And truly I am so vain, as to be so self-conceited or so naturally partial as to think my friends ·have as much reason to love me as another, since none can love more sincerely than I; and it were an injustice to prefer a fainter affection or to esteem the body more than the mind.* Likewise I

---

* The latter part of this sentence is obscure ; but, no doubt, the Duchess, in comparing herself with others who might profess superior claims to her friends' affection, means to deprecate any rival claims based on the ground of personal beauty.

am neither spiteful, envious nor malicious. I
repine not at the gifts that nature, or fortune
bestows upon others: yet I am a great emulator:
for, though I wish none worse than they are,
nor fear any should be better than they are,
yet it is lawful for me to wish myself the
best, and to do my honest endeavours there-
unto. I think it no crime to wish myself the
exactest of Nature's works, my thread of life
the longest, my chain of destiny the strongest,
my mind the peacablest, my life the pleasantest,
my death the easiest and myself the greatest
Saint in heaven: also to do my endeavour, so
far as honour and honesty doth allow of, to
be the highest on Fortune's wheel, and to hold
the wheel from turning, if I can. And if it be
commendable to wish another's good it were a
sin not to wish my own. For as envy is a
vice so emulation is a virtue; but emulation is
in the way to ambition—nay, it is a noble ambition. I fear my ambition inclines to vain-
glory; for I am very ambitious. Yet 'tis neither
for beauty, wit, titles, wealth or power, except
as they are steps to raise me to Fame's Tower,

which is to live by remembrance in after ages.
Likewise I am what the vulgar calls proud.
Not out of self-conceit or to slight or condemn
any, but scorning to do a base or mean act,
and disdaining rude or unworthy persons, insomuch that if I should find any that were rude
or too bold I should be apt to be so passionate
as to affront them, if I could, unless discretion
should get betwixt my passion and their boldness, which sometimes perchance it might, if
discretion should crowd hard for place. For
though I am naturally bashful, yet, in such a
cause, my spirits would be all on fire. Otherwise I am so well bred as to be civil to all
persons of all degrees or qualities. Likewise I
am so proud of or rather, just to my Lord, as
to abate nothing of the quality of his wife ; for
if honour be the mark of merit, and the royal
favour of his master, who will favour none but
those who have a merit to deserve,* it were a

----

* We may overlook the broad lie of the Duchess's
statement, in the hope that the distance of retirement
lent enchantment to her view of the Court. It is perhaps a

baseness for me to neglect the ceremony thereof. In some cases I am naturally a coward, in other cases very valiant. As for example, if any of my nearest friends were in danger I should never consider my life in striving to help them though I were sure to do them no good: and I would willingly nay cheerfully resign my life for their sakes. Likewise I should not spare my life if honour bid me die . . . . . Also as I am not covetous so I am not prodigal; but of the two I am inclining to be prodigal—I cannot say to a vain prodigality, because I imagine it is to a profitable end: for perceiving the world is given or apt, to honour the outside more than the inside, worshipping show more than substance, I am so vain (if it be a vanity) as to endeavour to be worshipped rather than not to be regarded. Yet I shall never be so prodigal

---

natural folly that, in speaking of her husband's honours, she should have deemed all who took them from the same fountain to have richly merited them ; while, earlier in this autobiography in speaking of her father's refusal of them, she should have despised the ' titles that were to be sold.'

as to impoverish my friends, or go beyond the
limits or facility of our estate. Though I desire
to appear at the best advantage, whilst I live in
the view of the public world, yet I could most
willingly exclude myself, so as never to see the
face of any creature but my Lord as long as I
lived; inclosing myself like an anchoret, wearing
a frieze gown, tied with a cord about my waist.

But I hope my Readers will not think me
vain for writing my life since there have been
many more that have done the like, as *Caesar*
and *Ovid* and many more both men and women;
and I know no reason I may not do it as
well as they. But I verily believe some cen-
suring Readers will scornfully say, ' Why hath
this Lady writ her own life? since none cares
to know whose daughter she was, or whose
wife she is, or how she was bred or what
fortunes she had, or what humour or disposition she was of?' I answer that it is true
that 'tis of no purpose to the Reader, but it is
to the Authoress. I write it for my own sake
not theirs. Neither did I intend this piece for
to delight but to divulge, not to please the fancy

but to tell the truth, lest after ages should mistake in not knowing I was daughter to one Master *Lucas* of *St John's* near *Colchester* in *Essex* and second wife to the Lord Marquis of *Newcastle;* for my Lord having had two wives, I might easily have been mistaken, especially if I should die and my Lord marry again.*

---

* This mistake, as Brydges points out, was actually made. In *The Loungers Common Place Book*, vol. ii. p. 398, there is a notice of the Duchess wherein this passage occurs. ‘This lady, the first of characters, a good wife, as well as a sensible and accomplished woman, was the daughter of William Bassett, Esquire, of an ancient family in the county of Stafford.’ The Lounger's morality is better and more curious than his information. The notice concludes thus: ‘It is not possible to view even her picture without admiration; such is the charm of moral and mental beauty, far more attractive and durable than the transient stimulus of a swelling bosom, auburn tresses and love-darting eyes’!

POEMS

BY

THE FIRST DUKE AND DUCHESS OF NEWCASTLE.

POEMS.

THE DUCHESS TO HER READERS.

A POET I am neither born nor bred,
But to a witty poet married:
Whose brain is fresh and pleasant as the Spring,
Where Fancies grow and where the Muses sing.
There oft I lean my head, and listening, hark,
To catch his words and all his fancies mark:
And from that garden show of beauties take
Whereof a posy I in verse may make.
Thus I, that have no gardens of my own,
There gather flowers that are newly blown.

AN APOLOGY FOR HER POETRY.

I language want to dress my fancies in,
The hair's uncurled, the garment's loose and thin.
Had they but silver lace to make them gay,
They'd be more courted than in poor array;
Or, had they art, would make a better show;
But they are plain; yet cleanly do they go.

The world in bravery doth take delight,
And glistering shows do more attract the sight :
And every one doth honour a rich hood,
As if the outside made the inside good.
And every one doth bow and give the place,
Not for the man's sake but the silver lace.
Let me intreat in my poor book's behalf,
That all will not adore the golden calf.
Consider, pray, gold hath no life therein,
And life, in nature, is the richest thing.
Be just, let Fancy have the upper place,
And then my verses may perchance find grace.

THE PASTIME OF THE QUEEN OF FAIRIES.*

[From ' *Poems and Fancies.*']

Queen Mab and all her Fairy fry,
Dance on a pleasant molehill high :
With fine straw pipes sweet music's pleasure,
They make and keep just time and measure.

---

* My corrections and alterations of this poem have been rather numerous. Parts of it are exceedingly clumsy and feeble.

All hand in hand, around, around,
They dance upon the Fairy ground.
And when she leaves her dancing-hall
She doth for her attendants call,
To wait upon her to a bower,
Where she doth sit beneath a flower,
To shade her from the moonshine bright ;
And gnats do sing for her delight.*
The whilst the bat doth fly about
To keep in order all the rout.
She on a dewy leaf doth bathe,
And as she sits the leaf doth wave :
Like a new fallen flake of snow
All her white limbs in beauty show.
Her garments fair her maids put on,
Made of the pure light from the sun,
From whence such colours she inshades
In every object she invades.
Then to her dinner she goes straight,
Where all her imps in order wait.

---

*   ' And now upon
The gnat's watchword the elves are gone.'
        HERRICK.

Upon a mushroom there is spread
A cover fine of spiders web :
And for her stool a thistle-down ;
And for her cup an acorn's crown,
Wherein strong nectar there is filled,
That from sweet flowers is distilled.
Flies of all sorts both fat and good,
For snipe, quail, partridge are her food.
Omelettes made of ant eggs new—
Of such high meats she eats but few.
Her milk is from the dormouse udder,
Which makes her cheese and cream and butter:
This they do mix in many a knack,
And fresh laid ants' eggs therein crack ;
Both pudding, custard and seed-cake,
Her skilled cook well knows how to bake.
To sweeten them the bee doth bring
Pure honey gathered by her sting :
But for her guard serves grosser meat—
They of the stall-fed dormouse eat.
When dined she calls, to take the air,
Her coach which is a nutshell fair ;
Lined soft it is and rich within,
Made of a glistering adders skin,

And there six crickets draw her fast,
When she a journey takes in haste:
Or else two serve to pace a round,
And trample on the Fairy ground.
To hawk sometimes she takes delight,
Her bird a hornet swift for flight,
Whose horns do serve for talons strong,
To gripe the partridge-fly among.
But if she will a hunting go,
The lizard answers for a doe;
It is so swift and fleet in chase,
That her slow coach cannot keep pace;
Then on the grasshopper she'll ride
And gallop in the forest wide.
Her bow is of a willow branch,
To shoot the lizard on the haunch :
Her arrow sharp, much like a blade,
Of a rosemary leaf is made.
Then home she's summoned by the cock,
Who gives her warning what's o'clock,
And when the moon doth hide her head,
Her day is done, she goes to bed.
Meteors do serve, when they are bright,
As torches do, to give her light,

Glow-worms for candles are lit up,
Set on the table while she sup.
But women, the inconstant kind,
Ne'er in one place content their mind,
She calls her chariot and away
To upper earth—impatient of long stay.

The stately palace in which the Queen dwells
Is a fabric built of hodmandod * shells:
The hangings thereof a rainbow that's thin,
Which shew wondrous fine as you enter in;
The chambers are made of amber that's clear
Which gives a sweet smell when fire is near:
Her bed is a cherry-stone carvèd throughout
And with a bright butterfly's wing hung about:
Her sheets are made of dove's eyes skin—
Her pillow's a violet bud laid therein :
The doors of her chamber are transparent glass,
Where the Queen may be seen as within she
    doth pass.
The doors are locked fast with silver pins;
The Queen is asleep and now man's day
    begins.

---

* Hodmandod.   A fish that casts its shell. like a
lobster or a crab.   A shell-snail called the dodman.

AN EPILOGUE TO THE ABOVE.

Sir Charles into my chamber coming in,
When I was writing of my ' Fairy Queen ;'
' I pray '—said he—' when Queen Mab you do see
Present my service to her Majesty :
And tell her I have heard Fame's loud report
Both of her beauty and her stately court.'
When I Queen Mab within my fancy viewed,
My thoughts bowed low, fearing I should be rude ;
Kissing her garment thin which fancy made,
I knelt upon a thought, like one that prayed ;
And then, in whispers soft, I did present
His humble service which in mirth was sent;
Thus by imagination I have been
In Fairy court and seen the Fairy Queen.

SORROW.

Upon a grave outrageous Sorrow sat,
Digging the earth as if she through would get ;
Her hair untied, loose on her shoulders hung,
And every hair with tears like beads was strung.

And as those tears fell fast with their own weight
Lo ! new-born tears supplied their places straight.
She held a dagger, seeming to be bold—
Grief bid her strike but fear did bid her hold.

Impatience raised her voice with shrieking shrill,
That sounded like a trumpet on a hill.
Her face was flecked like marble streaked with
        red,
Caused by grief's vapours flying to her head.
Her bosom bare, her garments loose and wide,
And thus she lay by Death's cold side.

By chance a man who had a fluent tongue,
Came walking by and saw her lie along ;
Pitying her sad condition and her grief,
He strove with rhetorick's help to give relief.

'Why do you mourn,' said he, 'and thus complain,
Since grief will neither Death nor Gods restrain ?
When they at first all creatures did create,
They gave them life to death predestinate.

Your sorrow cannot alter their decree,
Nor call back life this blind impatiency,
The dead cannot from love receive a heat
Nor hear the sound of lamentations great.

Then mourn no more since you no help can
    give :
Take pleasure in your beauty whilst you live ;
For in the fairest Nature pleasure takes,
And, if you die, Death double triumph makes.'

At last his words, like keys, unlocked her ears,
And then she straight considers what she hears.
' Pardon, you Gods !' said she, ' my murmuring
    crime,
My grief shall ne'er dispute your Will Divine,
But in sweet life will I take new delight'——
And so went home with that fond carpet knight.

SONG OF THE PRINCESS :

IN THE CHARACTER OF A SHEPHERD, WITH LADY HAPPY.

[From ' *The Convent of Pleasure.*']

My Shepherdess your wit flies high,
        Up to the sky,
And views the gates of heaven,
Which are the planets seven ;

Sees how fixed stars are placed
And how the meteors waste;
What makes the snow so white,
And how the sun breeds light;
What makes the biting cold
On everything take hold,
And hail, a mixt degree
'Twixt snow and ice; you see
From whence the winds do blow:
What thunder is, you know,
And what makes lightning flow
Like liquid flames, you show;
From sky you come to earth
And view each creature's birth,
Sink to the centre deep,
Where all dead bodies sleep;
And then observe to know
What makes the minerals grow;
How vegetables sprout,
And how the plants come out;
Take notice of all seed,
And what the Earth doth breed;
Then view the springs below,
And mark how waters flow;

What makes the tides to rise
Up proudly to the skies;
And shrinking back descend,
As fearing to offend;
Also your wit doth view
The vapour and the dew,
In summer's heat, that wet
Doth seem, like the Earth's sweat.
In winter time that dew
Like paint's white to the view:
Cold makes the thick-white, dry
As ceruse * it doth lie
On the earth's black face, so fair
As painted ladies are;
But when a heat is felt,
That frosty paint doth melt.

Thus Heaven and Earth you view,
And see what's old,—what's new;
How bodies transmigrate—
Lives are predestinate.
And with your wit reveal
What Nature would conceal.

---

* Ceruse : white lead.

  L. Happy. My shepherd,
All those who live do know it
That you are born a poet;
Your wit doth search mankind,
In body and in mind;
 The appetites you measure
And weigh each several pleasure;
Do figure every passion,
And every humour's fashion;
See how the fancy's wrought,
And what makes every thought;
Fathom conceptions low,
From whence opinions flow;
Observe the memory's length,
And understanding's strength;
Your wit doth reason find,
The centre of the mind,
Wherein the rational soul
Doth govern and control;
There doth she sit in state,
Predestinèd by fate
And by the Gods' decree
That sovereign she should be.
And thus your wit can tell,

How souls in bodies dwell;
As that the mind dwells in the brain,
And in the mind the soul doth reign,
That in the soul the life doth last,
For with the body it doth not waste;
Nor shall wit like the body die,
But live in the world's memory.*

THE CONVENT OF PLEASURE.

Lady Happy resolves to seclude herself from Mankind.

L. Happy. Men are the only troublers of women: for they only cross and oppose their sweet delights and peaceable life: they cause their pains but not their pleasures. Wherefore those women that are poor, and have not means to buy delights and maintain pleasures are only fit for men: for having not means

---

* Sir E. Brydges says that parts of this poem, though only in four feet verses, remind him of the manner of *Blackmore's Creation*, which was so strongly and hyperbolically commended by Dr. Johnson.

to please themselves they must serve only to please others. But those women, where Fortune, Nature and the Gods are joined to make them happy, were mad to live with men who make the female sex their slaves; but I will not be so enslaved but will live retired from their company. Wherefore in order thereto, I will take so many noble persons of my own sex as my estate will plentifully maintain, such whose births are greater than their fortunes, and as are resolved to live a single life and vow virginity: with these I mean to live encloistered with all the delights and pleasures that are allowable and lawful. My cloister shall not be a cloister of restraint, but a place for freedom, not to vex the senses but to please them.

> For every sense shall pleasure take,
> And all our lives shall merry make:
> Our minds in full delight shall joy,
> Not vex'd with every idle toy:
> Each season shall our caterers be,
> To search the land and fish the sea;

To gather fruit and reap the corn
That's brought to us in Plenty's horn:
With which we'll feast and please our taste,
But not, luxurious, make a waste.
We'll clothe ourselves with softest silk,
And linen fine as white as milk:
We'll please our sight with pictures rare,
Our nostrils with perfumèd air,
Our ears with soft melodious sound,
Whose substance can be nowhere found:
Our taste with sweet delicious meat,
And savoury sauces we will eat:
Variety each sense shall feed,
And changes shall new appetites breed.
Thus will in Pleasure's Convent I
Live with delight and with it die.

SONG BY LADY HAPPY.

As a Sea-Goddess.

My cabinets are oyster-shells,
In which I keep my Orient pearls:
And modest coral I do wear,
Which blushes when it touches air.

On silver waves I sit and sing,
And then the fish lie listening:
Then resting on a rocky stone
I comb my hair with fishes bone:

The whilst Apollo with his beams
Doth dry my hair from soaking streams,
His light doth glaze the water's face,
And make the sea my looking glass.

So when I swim on waters high,
I see myself as I glide by,
But when the sun begins to burn,
I back into my waters turn,

And dive unto the bottom low:
Then on my head the waters flow
In curlèd waves and circles round,
And thus with eddies I am crowned.*

SORROW'S TEARS.

Into the cup of Love pour Sorrow's tears,
Where every drop a perfect image bears,

---

* I have been obliged for the sake of both symmetry
and harmony to leave out several verses in this song.

And trickling down the hill of Beauty's cheek,
Fall on the breast, dive through, the heart to
    seek:
Which heart would be burnt up with fire of
    grief,
Did not those tears with moisture give relief.

A MAN TO HIS MISTRESS.

O do not grieve, Dear Heart, nor shed a tear,
Since in your eyes my life doth all appear;
And in your countenance my death I find;
I'm buried in your melancholy mind.

But in your smiles, I'm glorified to rise,
And your pure love doth me eternalize:
Thus by your favour you a god me make,
When in your hate a devil's shape I take.

THE FOUR SEASONS OF THE YEAR.

Although I am not rich in wit,
Nor know what tales your humours fit:
Yet now my young and budding muse
Will draw the seasons of the year,

Like prentice-painters which do use
The same, to make their skill appear.
But Nature is the hand to guide
The pencil of the mind, and place
The shadows so that they may hide
All the defects or give a grace.

The SPRING is dressed in buds and blossoms
    sweet,
And grass-green socks she draws upon her feet:
Of freshest air a garment she cuts out,
With painted tulips fringèd round about:
And lines it all within with violets blue
And yellow primrose of the palest hue.
She wears an apron made of lilies white,
And laced about with rays of dazzling light:
Cuffs of narcissus her fair hands do tie,
Pinned close with stings of bees which buzzing
    fly:
Ribbons of pinks and gilliflowers she makes,
Roses both white and red for knots she takes.
And when she's drest the birds in love do fall,
And chirping then do to each other call
To sing and hop and merry make
For the gentle sweet Spring's sake.

But of all birds the nightingale delights
To sing the Spring to bed in warmer nights;
And in the morning when asleep she lies
He sings again to make her rise,
And calls the sun to open her fair eyes,
Who gallops fast that he may her surprise.
But when the Spring is past her virgin prime,
And married is to bald old father Time:
The nightingale for grief doth cease to sing,
And silent is till comes another Spring.

The SUMMER's clothed in glorious sunshine bright
And with a trailing veil of long daylight :
Dry dust as powder on her hair doth place,
And with the morning dew doth wash her face.
A Zephyrus-wind she for a fan doth spread
To cool her cheeks which are hot-burning-red :
And with the heat so thirsty she doth grow,
That she drinks all the fresh sweet springs that
      flow.
Then in a thundering chariot she doth ride
To astonish mortals with her pride :
Bright-flashing lightning 'fore her flies,
A fluid fire that spreads about the skies.

And when she from her chariot doth alight
Then she is waited on by sunbeams bright.
Or else the rays that from the moon do spread
Like waxen tapers light her to her bed:
There with refreshing sleep short time to rest,
Breathing sweet zephyrs from her panting
    breast.
At high noon with the butterflies she'll play,
In twilight with the bats doth dance the hay:
Or, at the setting of the sun, will fly
With swallows swift in lively company.
But, if she's cross'd, she straight malicious grows,
And in a fury plagues on men she throws.
Of all the seasons of the year
She doth most full and fat appear:
Her blood is hot and flows with swelling tide,
She's only fit to be Apollo's bride:
But she, like other ladies in their prime,
Doth fade and wither at the breath of Time.

Autumn, although she's in her fading years,
And sober, yet in pleasant garb appears.
Her garments are not decked with flowers gay,
Nor are they green like those of maiden May;

But are the colour of the dapple deer,
Or hares that like a sandy ground appear.
Yet she is rich, with plenty doth abound,
All Earth's increase is in her satchel found.
She, to all Creatures nourishment doth give,
And by her bounty men, beasts, birds do live.
Besides the grievèd heart with joy doth fill
When from plump grapes the wine she doth distil.

Then Autumn glides away and leaves our sphere
To Winter cold at whom trees shake for fear:
And in that passion all their leaves do shed,
And all their sap back to the root is fled.
She comes apace with dark and lowering brow,
No pleasant recreations doth allow.
Her skin is wrinkled and her blood is cold,
Her flesh is numb, her hands can nothing hold:
Her face is swarthy and her eyes are red,
Her lips are blue and palsy shakes her head:
Her humour's sad and oft in showers she'll cry,
Or with loud storms in blustering passions fly.*

---

* Many lines have of necessity been omitted and varied
in this poem.

TIME.

TIME, an engraver, cuts the seal of Truth:
And as a painter draws both age and youth:
His colours mixed with oil of health lays on
The plump smooth cheek he pencils them upon:
Shadows of age he limns with sadder skill,
Making the hollow places darker still.

A DIALOGUE BETWEEN MELANCHOLY
AND MIRTH.

As I sat musing by myself alone,
My thoughts brought several things to work
    upon:
　　*　　　　*　　　　*　　　　*
At last came two which were in various dress,
One Melancholy, the other did Mirth express.
Melancholy was all in black array,
And Mirth was drest in colours fresh and gay.
Mirth laughing came and, running to me, flung
Her fat white arms about my neck and hung,
Embraced and kissed me oft and stroked my
    cheek,
Saying she would no other lover seek.

'I'll sing you songs and please you every day,
Invent new sports to pass the time away,
I'll keep your heart and guard it from that thief
Dull melancholy care, or sadder grief:
And make your eyes with mirth to overflow,
And full with springing blood your cheeks shall
    grow.
Your legs shall nimble be, your body light,
And all your spirits rise like birds in flight:
Mirth shall digest your meat and make you strong,
Shall give you health and your short days
    prolong.
Refuse me not but take me to your wife,
For I shall make you happy all your life.
If you take Melancholy, she'll make you lean,
Your cheeks shall hollow grow, your jaws be seen:
Your eyes shall buried be within your head,
You'll look as pale as if you were quite dead.
She'll make you start at every noise you hear
And visions strange shall in your eyes appear,
Your stomach cold and raw, digesting naught:
Your liver dry: your heart with sorrow fraught.
Thus would it be if you to her were wed,
But better far 'twould be that you were dead.

Her voice is low and gives a hollow sound:
She hates the light, in darkness only found:
Or set with blinking lamps or tapers small,
Which various shadows make against the wall.
She loves nought else but noise that discords
    make,
As croaking frogs which dwell down in the lake,
The raven's hoarse, the mandrake's hollow groan,
And shrieking owls in night which fly alone,
The tolling bell which for the dead rings out,
A mill where rushing waters run about,
The roaring winds which shake the cedars tall,
Plough up the seas and beat the rocks withal.
She loves to walk in the still moonshine night,
Where in a thick dark grove she takes delight.
In hollow cave, house thatched or lowly cell,
She loves to live and all alone to dwell.
Her ears are stopped with thoughts, her eyes
    purblind,
For all she hears or sees is in the mind.
(Though in her mind luxuriously she lives,
Imagination several pleasures gives).
Then leave her to herself alone to dwell,
Let you and I with mirth and pleasure swell,

And drink long, lusty draughts from Bacchus'
    bowl,
Until our brains on vaporous waves do roll;
Let's 'joy ourselves in amorous delights,
There's none so happy as the carpet knights!'

Melancholy with sad and sober face,
Complexion pale but of a comely grace,
With modest countenance, soft speech, thus
    spake:
'May I so happy be your love to take?
True, I am dull, yet by me you shall know
More of yourself—so wiser you shall grow.
I search the depth and bottom of mankind,
Open the eye of ignorance that's blind:
I travel far and view the world about,
I walk with Reason's staff to find Truth
    out:
I watchful am all dangers for to shun,
And do prepare 'gainst evils that may come:
I hang not on inconstant Fortune's wheel,
Nor yet with unresolving doubts do reel:
I shake not with the terror of vain fears,
Nor is my mind filled with unuseful cares:

I do not spend my time like idle Mirth,
Who only happy is just at her birth,
Who seldom lives so long as to be old,
And if she doth, can no affections hold;
For in short time she troublesome will grow:
Though at the first she makes a pretty show,
She makes a constant noise and keeps a rout,
And with dislike most commonly goes out.
Mirth good-for-nothing is, like weeds she grows,
Such plants cause madness Reason never knows.
Her face with laughter crumples in a heap,
Which ploughs large furrows—wrinkles long
      and deep:
Her eyes do water and her skin turns red,
Her mouth doth gape, teeth bared like one that's
      dead:
She fulsome is and gluts the senses all,
Offers herself and comes before a call;
Seeks company out and hates to be alone,
Unwelcome guests affronts are thrown upon.
Her house is built upon the golden sands,
Yet on no true and safe foundation stands;
A palace 'tis, where comes a great resort,
It makes a noise and gives a loud report.

Yet underneath the roof disasters lie
That oft beat down the house and many kill
    thereby.—

'I dwell in groves that gilt are with the sun,
Sit on the banks by which clear waters run;
In summers hot down in the shade I lie,
My music is the buzzing of a fly,
Which in the sunny beams doth dance all
    day,
And harmlessly doth pass the time away.
I walk in meadows soft with fresh green grass,
Or fields where corn is high, through which I
    pass,
Walk up the hills whence round I prospects see,
Where brushy woods and fairest champaigns be;
Returning back, in the fresh pasture go,
And hear the bleating sheep, the cows to low,
They gently feed, no evil think upon,
Have no designs to do each other wrong.
In winter cold when nipping frosts come on,
Then do I live in a small house alone;
Although 'tis plain yet cleanly 'tis within
Like to a soul that's pure and clear from sin.

And there I dwell in quiet and still peace,
Not filled with care my riches to increase;
I wish nor seek for vain and fruitless pleasures—
There is no wealth but what the Mind intreasures.
Thus am I solitary and live alone,
Yet better loved the more that I am known,
And though my face be ill favoured at first sight,
After acquaintance it shall give delight.
For I am like a shade; who sits in me
Shall not come wet, nor yet sun-burnèd be;
I keep off blustering storms from doing hurt,
When Mirth is often smutched with dust and
    dirt.
Refuse me not, for I shall constant be,
Maintain your credit and your dignity.

A DIALOGUE BETWEEN EARTH AND DARKNESS.

EARTH.

O horrid Darkness! and ye powers of Night!
Desponding shades made by obstructed light;
Why so perverse—What evil have I done?—
To part me from my Husband, the bright Sun?

DARKNESS.

I do not part you! He me hither sends,
Whilst he rides round to visit all his friends.
Besides he hath more wives to love than you,
He never to one constant is nor true!

EARTH.

You do him wrong, for though he journies make
For exercise—he care for me doth take.
He leaves the Stars his sisters in his place,
To comfort me while he doth run his race;
But you do come most wicked, thievish Night!
To rob me of their fair and silver light.

DARKNESS.

The Moon and Stars! they are but shadows thin!
Small cobweb-lawn they from His light do spin:
Which they in scorn do weave, you to disgrace,
As a thin veil to cover your ill face.
The Moon or Stars have no strong lights to show
A colour true, nor how you bud or grow,
Only some ghosts that rise and take delight
To flit about when the pale moon shines bright.

EARTH.

You are deceived—they cast no such disguise—
Strive me to please by twinkling in the skies.
As for the ghosts they are my children weak
And tender eyed, who the Moon's help do seek.
For why?   Her light so gentle, moist and cold
Doth ease their eyes when they do it behold.
But you with shadows' fright delude the sight,
Like Death appear, with gloomy shades of night.
And, with thick clouds, you cast upon my back
A mourning mantle of the deepest black,
Which covers me with deep obscurity,
That none of my dear children I can see,
Their lovely faces masking from my sight,
Which show most beautiful in the day-light;
They take delight to view, and to adorn,
And fall in love with one another's form.
By which kind sympathy they bring me store
Of children young, those growing up bring
    more.
But you, so spiteful to those loves so kind,
Muffling their faces, make their eyes quite
    blind!

DARKNESS.

Is this my thanks for all my love and care,
And for the great respect to you I bear?
I am thy kindly, true and constant lover,
I all thy faults and imperfections cover,
I take you in my gentle arms of rest,
With cool fresh dews I bath your heated breast,
The children which you by the Sun did bear
I lay to sleep and lull them from their care.
On beds of silence soft I wrap them in,
And cover them with blankets black, yet clean,
And shut them close from the disturbing light,
And yet you rail against your lover Night!
Why if you had the light through all the year,
Beauty though great would not so well appear,
For what is common has not such respect,
Nor much regard—for use doth bring neglect;
Nought is admired but what is seldom seen,
And black for change, delights as well as green.
I should most constant be if I might stay,
But the bright Sun doth beat me quite away.
For he is active and runs all about,
Nor dwells with one but seeks new lovers out,

He spiteful is to other lovers since
He by his light doth give intelligence.
But I Love's confidant am made; I bring
Them to my shade to meet and whisper in.
Thus am I faithful—kind to lovers true—
And all is for the sake and love of you!
What though I'm melancholy? my love's as strong
As the great Light's that you so dote upon.
Then slight me not nor do my suit disdain,
But when the Sun is gone me entertain.
Take me sweet Earth with joy unto your bed
And on your fresh green breast lay my black
    head.

A LADY DRESSED BY YOUTH.

Her hair was curls of Pleasure and Delight,
Which on her brow did cast a glistening light.
As lace her bashful eyelids downward hung:
A modest countenance o'er her face was flung:
Blushes, as coral beads, she strung to wear
About her neck, and pendants for each ear:
Her gown was by Proportion cut and made,
With veins embroidered, with complexion laid,

Rich jewels of pure honour she did wear,
By noble actions brightened everywhere :
Thus dressed, to Fame's great court straightways
    she went,
To dance a brawl with Youth, Love, Mirth,
    Content.

A WOMAN DRESSED BY AGE.

A milkwhite fillet bound up all her hairs,
And a deaf coif did cover both her ears :
A sober countenance on her face she ties,
And a dim sight doth muffle half her eyes :
About her neck's a kercher of coarse skin,
That Time hath crumpled and worn creases in :
Her gown was turned to melancholy black,
And loose did hang upon her sides and back :
Her stockings cramp had knit : red-worsted gout
And pains as garters tied her legs about :
A pair of palsy gloves her hands draw on,
With weakness stitched and numbness trimmed
    upon :
A mantle of diseases laps her round :
And thus she's drest for Death to lay i' th' ground.

THE FUNERAL OF CALAMITY.

Calamity was laid on *Sorrow's* hearse
And coverings had of melancholy verse :
Compassions as kind friends, do mourning go
And tears about the corpse as flowers strow.
A garland of deep sighs by *Pity* made
Was on the sad bier laid :
Bells of *Complaints* did ring it to the grave
And *History* a monument of fame it gave.

THE FUNERAL OF TRUTH.

Truth in the Golden Age was healthy, strong,
But in the Silver Age grew lean and wan :
I' th' Brazen Age sore-sick abed did lie :
And in the last hard Iron Age did die.
Measuring and *Reckoning*, both being just,
She as her two executors did trust,
Her goods for to distribute all about
To her dear friends, as legacies giv'n out.
Mourning she gave to all her friends to wear,
And did appoint that four her hearse should
    bear :

Love at the head did hold the winding-sheet,
On each side *Care* and *Fear*—*Sorrow* the feet;
This sheet at every corner fast was tied,
Made of oblivion strong and very wide.
Natural Affections in mourning clad,
Went next the hearse, with grief distracted mad :
And tore their hair, scratched faces, hands did
　　wring,
While from their eyes fountains of tears did
　　spring.
For *Truth*, said they, did always with us live,
Now that She's dead there's no trust we can
　　give.
Next them came *Honour* in garments black and
　　long,
With blubbered face and heavy head down hung;
Who wished to die, for life was now a pain—
Since *Truth* was dead, *Honour* no more could
　　gain.
After came *Kings* who all good laws did make,
And used their power for *Truth* and *Virtue's* sake.
Lovers, next these, with faces pale as death,
With shame-faced eyes, quick pulse and shortened
　　breath,

Who in each hand a bleeding heart did bring
And these into the grave of *Truth* did fling.
(And ever since lovers inconstant prove,
They more professions give than real love.)
Next them came *Counsellors* of all degrees
From courts and countries and renowned cities :
Their wise heads were a guard and a strong
    wall
So long as *Truth* did live amongst them all.
Some *Judges* came — no wrangling *Lawyers*
    base—
For *Truth* alive did plead and try each case ;
All sorts of *Tradesmen*, using not to swear
So long as Truth, not oaths, sold off their
    ware ;
Widows, that to their husbands kind had swore
That, if they died, they'd never marry more.
At last the *Clergy* came who taught Truth's
    way
And how men in devotion ought to pray :
By moral laws the lives of men direct,
Persuade to peace, and governor's respect.
They, bathed in grief, as prophets did fortell
That all the world to *Falsehood* would rebel.

Faction will come, said they, and bear great
    sway,
And bribery shall the innocent betray :
Controversies within the Church shall rise,
And Heresy shall bear away the prize.
Instead of peace the priests shall discords preach,
And high rebellion in their doctrines teach :
Then shall men learn the statutes to explain,
Which learning only serves for lawyers' gain :
For they do make and spread them in a net
To take in clients and their money get.
The laws which wise men made to keep the
    peace,
Serve only then for quarrels to increase :
And those that sit on *Honour's* stately throne
Be counterfeits, nor any genuine known ;
They put on vizards of an honest face,
But all their acts unworthy be and base :
Friendship in words and compliments will live,
Not one night's lodgings in the heart will give :
Lovers shall die for lust yet love not one,
And *Virtue* unregarded sit alone.
Now *Truth* is dead no *Goodness* here will dwell,
But fell *Disorder* make each place a hell.

With that they all shriek out, lament and cry
To *Nature* that she'd end their misery.
But now this Iron Age's so rusty grown,
Our hearts are flint and care not where Truth's
     gone.

POETS AND THEIR THEFT.

As birds to hatch their young do sit in spring,
The ages do their broods of poets bring,
Who to the world in verse do sweetly sing.

Their notes great Nature set, not Art so taught:
For fancies in the brain by Nature wrought
Are best: what Imitation makes are nought:

For though they sing as well as well may be,
And make their notes of what they learn agree,
Yet he that teaches still hath mastery:

And ought to have the crown of praise and fame,
In the long roll of Time to write his name—
And, those that steal it out, but win the blame.

There's none should places have in Fame's high
    court,
But those who first do win Invention's fort,
Not messengers—that only make report.

To messengers reward of thanks are due
For their great pains to bring their message true,
But not the honour of invention new.

Many there are that suits will make to wear,
Of several patches stolen here and there,
That to the world they gallants may appear.

And the poor vulgar, who but little know,
Do reverence all that makes a glistering show,
Examining not the same how they came to.

FANCY AND PHRASE.

Most of our writers now a days,
Consider not the fancy but the phrase:
As if fine words were wit or one should say
A woman's handsome, if her clothes be gay:
Regarding not what beauty's in the face,
Nor what proportion doth the body grace;

As, when her shoes be high to say she's tall,
And when she's straight-laced to declare she's
    small;
When painted, or her hair is curled with art,
Though of itself but plain and her skin swart—
We cannot say from her a thanks is due
To nature; nor those arts in her we view,
Unless she them invented, and so taught
The world to set forth that which is stark nought.
But Fancy is the eye gives life to all,
Words the complexion—as a whited wall:
Fancy the form is, flesh, blood, skin and bone,
Words are but shadows, substance they have
    none:
But number is the motion, gives the grace,
And is the countenance of a well-formed face.

AN ELEGY UPON THE DEATH OF MY BROTHER.

Dear Brother,
        Thy idea in my mind doth lie,
And is entombed in my sad memory,

Where every day I to thy shrine do go,
And offer tears, which from mine eyes do flow;
My heart the fire, whose flames are ever pure,
Shall on Love's altar last while life endure;
My sorrow incense strews of sighs fetched deep,
My thoughts keep watch o'er thy sweet spirit's
    sleep.
Dear blessed soul though thou art gone yet lives
Thy fame on earth and man thee praises gives:
But all's too small: for thy heroic mind
Was above all the praises of mankind.

THE DEVIL TO BE AFRAID OF.

Women and fools fear in the dark to be,
Lest they the Devil in some shape should see:
As if, like silly owls, he takes delight
To sleep all day, and go abroad at night
To beat the pots and pans, and lamps blow out,
And all the night keep up a revel rout:
To make the sow to grunt, the pigs to squeak,
The dogs to bark, cats mew as if they speak:
Alas! poor Devil whose power is so small!
Only to make a cat or dog to bawl,

And with the hollow pewter make a noise,
To stew with fearful sweat poor girls and boys!
Why should we fear him since he doth no harm?
For we may bind him fast within a charm.
Then what a'devil ails a woman old
To play such tricks and give away her soul?
Can he destroy mankind or new worlds make,
Or alter states for an old woman's sake?
Or put the daylight out, or stop the sun,
Or draw the planets from their course to run?
And yet methinks 'tis sad and very strange
That since the Devil cannot bodies change,
He hath such power over souls, to draw
Them from their God and from his holy law.
Persuading conscience to perform more ill,
Than the sweet grace of God, to rule the will:
To cut off Faith, by which our souls should climb
Above, and leave our folly and our crime:
Destroying honesty, disgracing truth.
For though he cannot make old age nor youth:
Nor can he add or make a minute short:
Yet many souls he keeps from Heaven's court.
It seems his dreadful power forever lasts,
Because 'tis on the soul which never wastes.

And thus hath God the Devil power lent,
To punish man, unless he doth repent.

MAN'S SHORT LIFE AND FOOLISH AMBITION.

In gardens sweet each flower mark did I,
How they did spring, bud, blow, wither and die.

With that, contemplating of man's short stay,
Saw man like to those flowers pass away.

Yet built he houses, thick and strong and high,
As if he'd live to all Eternity.

Hoards up a mass of wealth, yet cannot fill
His empty mind, but covet will he still.

To gain or keep, such falsehood will he use !
Wrong, right or truth—no base ways will refuse.

I would not blame him could he death out keep,
Or ease his pains or be secure of sleep :

Or buy Heaven's mansions—like the gods become,
And with his gold rule stars and moon and sun :

Command the winds to blow, seas to obey,
Level their waves and make their breezes stay.

But he no power hath unless to die,
And care in life is only misery.

This *care* is but a word, an empty sound,
Wherein there is no soul nor substance found;

Yet as his heir he makes it to inherit,
And all he has he leaves unto this spirit.

To get this Child of Fame and this bare word,
He fears no dangers, neither fire nor sword:

All horrid pains and death he will endure,
Or any thing can he but fame procure.

O man, O man, what high ambition grows
Within his brain, and yet how low he goes!

To be contented only with a sound,
Wherein is neither peace nor life nor body found.

A HYMN TO DEITY.

Great God; from Thee all infinites do flow
And by thy power from thence effects do grow!

Thou orderest all degrees of matter; just
As 'tis thy will and pleasure move it must.
Thou by thy knowledge orderest all the best
For in thy knowledge doth thy wisdom rest;
And wisdom cannot order things amiss
For where disorder is, no wisdom is.
Besides great God, thy will is just, for why?
Thy will still on thy wisdom doth rely.
O pardon Lord for what I now here speak
Upon a guess, my knowledge is but weak;
But Thou hast made such creatures as mankind
And gav'st them something which we call a mind,
Always in motion, never quiet it lies
Unless the figure of his body dies.
His several thoughts, which several motions are
Do raise love, hope, joy, doubt and fear.
As love doth raise up hope, so fear doth doubt
Which makes him seek to find the great God out;
Self-love doth make him seek to find if he
Came from or shall last to eternity.
But motion being slow makes knowledge weak
And then his thoughts gainst ignorance do break.
As fluid waters gainst hard rocks do flow,
Break their soft streams and so they backward go,

Just so do thoughts: and then they backward slide
Unto the place where first they did abide,
And there in gentle murmurs do complain
That all their care and labour is in vain.
But since none knows, the great Creator must;
Men seek no more but in His greatness trust. *

---

* This Hymn, which occurs at the end of one of her strange 'philosophical' books, is curious as almost the only devotional passage to be found in the writings of the Duchess.

MISCELLANEOUS POEMS

MISCELLANEOUS POEMS.

I.

THOUGH BEAUTY wither and decay
　　Wisdom and Wit may in the ruin stay :
If youth doth waste, and life's oil's spent,
Yet Fame lasts long and builds a monument.
A melancholy life doth shadows cast,
But sets forth virtue, if they are well placed.
Then who would entertain an idle mirth,
　　Begot by Vanity, and die in scorn ?
Be proud, or pleased with beauty, when the birth
　　Becomes the grave or tomb as soon as born ?
But Wisdom wishes to be old and glad,
When youthful follies die or seem as mad.
Though age is subject to repent the past,
Prudence and virtue may redeem what's lost.

K

II.

LOVE, how thou'rt tired out with rhyme !
    Thou art a tree whereon all poets climb;
And from thy branches every one takes some
Of thy sweet fruit, which Fancy feeds upon.
But now thy tree is left so bare and poor,
That they can hardly gather one plum more.

III.

GIVE me that Wit whose fancy's not confined,
    That buildeth on itself, not two brains
        joined :
(For that's like oxen yoked and forced to draw,
Or like two witnesses for one deed, in law).
But's like the sun that needs no help to rise :
·Or like a bird, in air that freely flies :
Or like the sea which runneth round without,
And grasps the earth with twining arms about :
Thus true born Wit to others strength may
    give,
Yet by its own and not another's live.

IV.

GREAT Nature doth enfold the Soul within
  A fleshly garment which the Fates do spin.
And when the garments are grown old and bare,
With sickness torn, Death takes them off with
  care,
And folds them up in Peace and quiet Rest ;
So lays them safe within an earthly chest.
Then scours and makes them sweet and clean
Fit for the Soul to put them on again.

V.

THE Sun crowns Nature's head with splendent
  bars,
And in her hair as jewels hang the stars :
Her garments made of pure bright watchet skies,
The zodiack round her waist those garments ties,
The polar circles bracelets for her wrist,
The planets round about her neck are twist :
The gold and silver mines shoes for her feet,
And for her garters flowers soft and sweet :
Her stockings are of grass that's fresh and green ;
And rainbow ribbons, many colours in :

The powder for her hair is milkwhite snow,
And when she combs her locks the winds do
    blow:
Light a thin veil doth hang upon her face,
Through which her creatures see in every place.

VI.

I HATE your fools for they my brains do
    crack,
And when they speak put patience on the rack.
Their actions all from reason quite do run,
Their ends prove bad since ill they're first begun.
They fly from Wisdom—do her counsels fear,
As if she ruin to their heads brought near.
They seek a shadow—let the substance go,
And what is good or best they do not know:
Yet stiff in their opinions, stubborn, strong
Although you bray them, sayeth Solomon.
As spiders' webs entangle little flies
So fools wrapt up in webs of error lies:
Then comes the spider, flies with poison fills,
So mischief in their errors oft fools kills.

VII.

'TIS strange
How we do change!
First to live and then to die
Is a great misery!
To give us sense great pains to feel:
To make our lives to be Death's wheel:
To give us sense and reason too,
Yet know not what we're made to do:
And senses which like hounds do run about.
Yet never can the perfect truth find out.
O Nature! Nature! cruel to mankind,
Who gives us knowledge, misery to find!

VIII.

VIRTUES are several paths which lead to
heaven;
And they which tread these paths have graces
given:
Repentant tears allay the dust of pride;
And pious sighs do blow vain thoughts aside:
Sorrow and grief which in the heart do lie,
Do cloud the mind as thunder doth the sky:

But when in thundering groans it breaketh out
The mind grows clear, the sun of joy peeps
    out !
This pious life I now resolve to lead,
That in my soul doth joy and comfort breed.

IX.

WISE age majestic seems like gods above,
    Their countenance is mercy joined with
        love ;
Their silver hairs are like to glorious rays,
Their eyes, like monarch's sceptre, power sways,
Their life is justice' seat where judgments sit
Their tongue is the sharp sword which truth
    doth whet ;
Their grave behaviour's balances do poise
The scales of thought and action without noise ;
Merits the grains which make them even weight,
And honesty the hand that holds them straight.

X.

NOTHING was left but black despair,
    And grim Death in their eyes to stare :
For every gust of wind blew death into their face
And every billow digged their burial place.

POEMS BY THE DUKE

POEMS BY THE DUKE.

A WASSAIL SONG.

THE jolly wassail now do bring,
With apples drowned in strongest ale,
And freshest syllabubs, and sing;
Then each to tell their love-sick tale:
So home by couples and thus draw
Ourselves by holy Hymen's law.

PEDLER'S SONG.*

[From ' *The Triumphant Widow.*']

Come maids what is it that you lack?
I have many a fine knack
For you in my pedler's pack;
Your sweethearts then kindly smack,
If they freely will present you,
And with trinkets will content you.

Brushes, combs of tortoise shell,
For your money I will sell;

---

* Compare with Autolycus in ' *Winter's Tale.*'

Cambric lawn as white as milk,
Taffeta as soft as silk :
Garters rich with silver roses,
Rings with moral, divine posies :

Rainbow ribbons of each colour,
No walking shop ere yet was fuller ;
Various points and several laces
For your bodies' straight embraces :
Silver bodkins for your hair,
Bobs which maidens love to wear :

Here are pretty tooth-pick cases,
And the finest Flanders laces,
Cabinets for your fine doxies,
Stoppers and tobacco boxes,
Crystal Cupid's-looking-glasses,
Will enamour all your lasses :

Fine gilt prayerbooks, catechisms,
What is orthodox or schisms,
Or for loyal faith defendant—
Presbyter or Independent.
Ballads fresh for singing new,
And more, the ballads all are true !

A LIMBO.

In my love's despair I fell
Down to that furnace we call hell:
.The first strange thing that I did mark
Was many fires, and yet 'twas dark:
Instead of costly arras there
The walls poor sooty hangings wear;
Spirits went about each room
With pans of sulphur for perfume,
Sod tender ladies in a pot
For broths and jellies they had got;
Their spits well loaded with poor sinners
That devils roasted for their dinners;
While some were frying damnèd souls,
Others made rashers on the coals;
The waiting-women they did stew
That robbed their ladies of their due;
Gammons of usurers down were taken
That hung i' the chimney for their bacon.
Here lawyers baked in ovens stand,
For cozening clients of their land;

Millions of souls beyond expressing,
French devils tortured in the dressing.
To cool them there they drunk instead
Of beer huge draughts of molten lead;
Burnt claret they do never lack,
And all their spanish is mulled sack.
In throngs where new-come sinners stood
A reverend lady lost her hood;
A chamber-maid cried out 'Alas!
A devil had broke her looking-glass.'
A merchant cried burnt was his stuff,
A city wife had singed her muff;
A purchaser did howling cry—
'Alas! his deeds and seals did fry.'
A courtier lost his periwig
A hector lost his looking big;
The drunkards that were in the rout
At last did puke the fires out;
Hell being spoiled I came away,
And sinners now make holiday.*

---

* I print this as one of the most curious and ingenious of profane pieces that I know, and one not without a dash of wholesome satire in it.

LOVE'S OINTMENT.

[From ' *The Humorous Lovers.*']

CUPID AND VENUS, LOQ.

CUPID.   Dear Mother, powerful charms I've got
   A Lover's sighs—

VENUS.   —put them in the pot.

CUPID.   His groans, sad thoughts and his despair,
   His soul departed, turned to air.

VENUS.   Gently infused we'll boil them all
   In tears which his sad eyes let fall.

CUPID.   But Lady Venus, my dear mother,
   To make it stronger, here's another ;
   The Lover's feverish panting heart,
   Blood that did backward from it start,
   Cold sweats wrung through his porous
    skin,
   When to despair he did begin.

VENUS.   Cupid, I prithee my dear Son,
   Make what haste, thou canst, to 'have
    done.

CUPID.   Here's a bracelet of *her* hair,
   Beams that used to flow i' th' air,

Smiles that from her face did rise,
Glances shot from her bright eyes;
Coral from her lips too with
Shavèd ivory from her teeth;
From each vein a violet,
A strawberry from either teat,
Lilies took from her white skin,
Roses from her cheeks. All's in,
But the pot methinks too narrow.

VENUS. Stir the ingredients with thine arrow,
Thus Love's ointment we compound,
In which we dip the darts that wound.

SONG.

[From ' *The Humorous Lovers.*']

I.

From their bright celestial sphere
Venus and her son appear,
Gently descending to the earth
To give our loves a timely birth.

II.

In the fairest ladies' eyes
Cupid's fatal quiver lies;

From them he borrows all those darts
With which he wounds poor mortals' hearts.

III.

And man, alas, has no defence
Against an arrow taken thence !
Love's sweet infection seizes all,
The grief is epidemical.

SONG.

[From the same.]

We'll, placed in Love's triumphant chariot high,
Be drawn by milkwhite turtles through the sky,
And have for footmen Cupids running by.

A poet coachman, with celestial fire—
His gentle whip of melting pure desire—
Shall drive us while I do thy eyes admire.

Imperial laurel deck our temples round !
As victors, or as heated poets crowned,
Scorning to have commerce with the dull ground.

Thus we will drive o'er mighty hills of snow,
Viewing poor mortal lovers there below,
Wretches alas ! that know not where we go.

AN AERIAL FEAST.

(AN EXTRAVAGANZA.)

[From 'The Humorous Lovers'.]

Unto a feast I will invite thee
Where various dishes shall delight thee,
The steaming vapours drawn up hot
From Earth, that's Nature's porridge-pot,
Shall be our broth; we'll drink my dear
The thinner air form our small beer;
And if thou likest I'll call loud
And make our butler broach a cloud.
We'll of pale planets for thy sake
White-pots and trembling custards make:
The twinkling stars shall to our wish
Make a grand salad in a dish;
Snow for our sugar shall not fail,
Fine candied ice, comfits of hail;
For oranges gilt clouds we'll squeeze,
The milky-way we'll turn to cheese;
Sunbeams we'll catch to stand in place
Of hotter ginger, nutmegs, mace;
Sunsetting clouds for roses sweet,
And violet skies strewed for our feet;
The spheres shall for our music play,

While spirits dance the time away.
When we drink healths Jove shall be proud—
Th' old cannoneer—to fire a cloud,
That all the gods may know our mirth,
And trembling mortals too on earth.
And when our feasting shall be done
I'll lead thee uphill to the sun
And place thee there that thy eyes may
Add greater lustre to the day.

SONG.

[From ' *The Triumphant Widow.*']

I dote, I dote, but am a sot to show it,
I was a very fool to let her know it,
For now she doth so cunning grow
She proves a friend worse than a foe;
She'll neither hold me fast nor let me go!
She tells me I cannot forsake her so

If to leave late I ever endeavour,
    She to make me stay
    Throws a kiss in my way
O then I could tarry for ever.

But good madam Fickle be faithful,
And leave off your damnable dodging,
  Either love me or leave me
  And do not deceive me
But let me go home to' my lodging.

A MODEL HUSBAND.

[From ' *The Triumphant Widow.*']

Lady.—I am resolved never to marry
Till I can find a man of noble blood
With virtues greater than his pedigree :
One that fears nothing but to do a wrong,
Remembering everything but injuries :
Who has courage beyond a lion in his pride,
Yet hides that courage in his gentle breast :
That's just for justice' sake and one that weighs
All things in judgment's balance: with clear sight
Can hit the mark of men and business :
That prudently foresees from what is past :
. Hath wit as good as all the Roman poets :
With fancy quick and sharp, yet not offensive,
His discourse clear and short and what's his own :
Easy and natural on all occasions :
Of nature excellent—a melting soul
Ready t' oblige all mankind were 't in his power.

SERENADE.

[From ' *The Variety*,' a comedy.]

I conjure thee, I conjure thee by thy skin that
     is so fair,
   Thy dainty curlèd hair,
   And thy frown and thy grace,
   With the patches on thy face,
   And thy hand that doth invite
   The coldest, dullest appetite,
         Appear, appear !

If not so I do not care,
Though thy breasts be ne'er so bare,
Roses rich, with shoe that's white,
Or thou Venus' best delight;
   If not touch thy softer skin
   What care I for thee a pin ?
         Appear, appear!

For to hear and not to see,
Is a dull, flat history :
And to see and not to touch :
If you think the last too much—
   Know all woman's but one toy
   If we cannot them enjoy;
         Appear, appear !

SONG.

[From ' *The Variety,*' a comedy.]

Thine eyes to me like suns appear,
  Or brighter stars, their light;
Which makes it summer all the year
  Or else a day of night;
But truly I do think they are
But eyes, and neither sun nor star.

Thy brow is as the milky way,
  Whereon the gods might trace *;
Thy lips ambrosia I dare say
  Or nectar of thy face;
But to speak truly I do vow
They are but women's lips and brow.

Thy cheek it is a mingled bath
  Of lilies and of roses;
But here there's no man power hath
  To gather love's fresh posies;
Believe it, here the flowers that bud
Are but a woman's flesh and blood.

* Used here in the sense of drive or walk.

Thy nose a promontory fair,
  Thy neck a fairy land !
At nature's gifts so rarely rare
  All men amazed do stand ;
But to a clearer judgment those
Are but a woman's neck and nose.

Four lines in passion I can die
  As is the lover's guise ;
And dabble too in poetry
  Whilst love-possest ; then wise
As greatest statesmen or as those
Who know love best yet live in prose.

ELEGY.

[From ' *Nature's Pictures drawn by Fancies Pencil.*']

Titan, I banish all thy joys of light,
Turning thy glorious rays to gloomy night :
Clothing my chamber with sad black, each part
Thus suitable unto my mournful heart :
Only a dim wax taper there shall wait
On me, to shew my dark, unhappy fate.

With sorrowing thoughts my head shall furnish'd
    be,
And all my breath sad sighs, for love of thee ;
My groans to grieving notes be set with skill,
And sung in tears : and melancholy still
Languishing music to fill up each voice
With palsied, trembling strings be all my choice.

HEAVY GRIEF.

[From the play of ' *Bell in Campo*,' by the Duchess.]

LADY JANTIL *at her husband's tomb, putting off her
rich garments and ornaments, speaks thus :*

Now I depose myself and here lay down
Titles, not Honour, with my golden crown :
This crimson velvet mantle I throw by—
There ease and plenty in rich ermines lie !
Off with this glittering gown which once did bear
Ambition and fond pride !   Lie you all there !
Cut off these dangling tresses, once a crime
Urging my glass to look away the time !
Thus all those worldly vanities I waive
And bury them in my dear Husband's grave.

*She then calls for a pure white silk robe, loose and
girt about with a white silk cord, and a thin
black veil, and, as they are putting these on,
taking a book in her hand, says:*

Put on that pure and spotless garment white,
To show my chaster thoughts my soul delight:
Cord of humility about my waist—
A veil of mourning round me cast—
Here by this saddening tomb shall be my station,
And in this book my holy contemplation.

To her servants:

Farewell my sisters, farewell every one,
As you all love me pray leave me alone.

*They go forth weeping.—
When they are gone she turns to the tomb:*

No dust shall on thy marble ever stay,
But with my sadder sighs I'll blow it away:
And the least spot that any pillar bears,
I'll wash it clean with grief of dropping tears:
Sun, fly this hemisphere, and feast my eyes
With melancholy night, and never rise!
The twinkling stars that in cold nights are seen,
Clouds muster up and hide them as a screen!

As you, my Mother Earth, may nothing wear
But snow and icicles to curl your hair:
So may Dame Nature, barren, nothing bring—
Let all be chaos whence despair's a spring:
Since all my joys are gone what shall I do,
But wish the whole world ruined with me too.

ANOTHER SOLILOQUY.

[From the same.]

Lady Jantil.   So! 'Tis well!
Oh, Death hath shaked me kindly by the hand,
To bid me welcome to the silent grave.
'Tis dead and numb sweet Death! How thou
   dost court me!
O let me clap thy fallen cheeks with joy,
And kiss the emblem of what once was lips!
Thy hollow eyes I am in love withal,
And thy bald head beyond Youth's best-curled
   hair.
Prithee, embrace me in thy colder arms,
And hug me there to fit me for thy mansion:
Then bid our neighbour worms to feast with us,
Thus to rejoice upon my holiday.

—But thou art slow ! I prithee, hasten Death !
And linger not my hopes thus with thy stay.
' 'Tis not thy fault,' thou sayest ? ' but fearful
    Nature
That hinders thus thy progress in this way ?'
Oh foolish Nature, think'st thou canst withstand
Death's conquering and inevitable hand ?
Let me have music for divertisement !
This is my mask, Death's ball, my soul to dance
Out of her frail and fleshly prison here.
Oh, cold I now dissolve and melt ! I long
To free my soul in slumbers with a song !
In soft and quiet sleep here as I lie,
Steal gently out O Soul and let me die !

DEATH SONG : OF LADY INNOCENCE.

[From ' *Youth's Glory and Death's Banquet*,' a play by the
Duchess.]

    Life is trouble at the best,
    And in it we find no rest;
    Joys are all with sorrows crowned,
    No quietness till in the ground.

Man vexes man we still do find
He is the torture of his kind:
False man I scorn thee in my grave!
Come Death! I call thee as my slave.

FUNERAL SONG; BY VIRGINS.

[From the same.]

Spotless virgins, as you go,
Wash each step as white as snow
With pure crystal streams that rise
From the fountains of your eyes.

Fresher lilies, like the day,
Strew, and roses white as they:
For an emblem to disclose
This flower sweet, short-lived as those.

SONG.

[From ' *The Public Wooing*,' a play by the Duchess.]

Envious ladies now repine,
        Since you are crost
        In having lost
A Prince so handsome and so fine.

Mourn in black patches for your sins
  Discard each curl
  And every purl *
And throw away your dressing pins.

Lay by your gaudy gowns of state,
  For now you'll faint,
  For all your paint,
To think of your unhappy fate.

For these love pitfalls now are stale,
  And all despise
  Your glancing eyes;
For all forced arts in love will fail.

Now let your specious gilding pass;
  Your lips be fed
  With biting red,
Despair and break each looking-glass !

THE BEGGAR'S MARRIAGE.

Whilome there was a ragged beggar old,
Who in his time full fourscore winters told:

---

* Purl : an embroidery or lace,—puckered or *purfled*.

His head all froz'n, beard long and white as snow,
Propped with a staff, for else he could not go:
With blearèd eyne, all parchèd dry and cold,
With palsy shaking little could he hold.
On's cloak more patches there did stick
Than Algebra's arithmetic
Could once tell how to number, and was fuller
Than was the rainbow of each various colour.
His turf house leaned to an old stump of oak,
A hole at top there for to void the smoke.
A withered beggar-woman was there little sundered
From him, who, all the town said, was a hundred:
Toothless she was, nay more, worn all her gums,
And all her fingers too were gone to thumbs:
Wrinkles, deep graves to bury all delight,
Eyes now sunk holes that little had of sight:
Seldom she heard, sometimes, the great town-bell:
Little could speak, as little sense could tell.

A long forgetfulness her legs had seized,
For many years her crutches them had eased:
Clothes, thousand rags torn with the wind and
          weather,
Her housewifery long since had sewn together.

In a hot summer's day these out did creep,
Enlivened just like flies to leave their sleep,
And then Apollo's masterpiece did aim
To light dead-ashes' sparks—not make a flame.
Now heat and kindness made him try to kiss
    her,
But her old head so shook he oft did miss her :
He thought it modesty, she, gainst her will,
Striving to please him, could not hold it still.
She mumbled but he could not understand her :
He cried ' Sweet Hero I'll be thy Leander !'
She said : ' Before we met cold as a stone is
I was, but now am Venus, you Adonis.'
Such heights of passion's love uttered these two
As youngest lovers when they 'gin to woo :
For Cupid still his reign o'er man will have,
He governs from the cradle to the grave.
Their virtue's such they will not sin or tarry,
So, heated, vowed a contract then to marry.

This marriage now divulged was everywhere
To neighb'ring beggars, beggars far and near :
The day appointed and the marriage set,
The lame, the blind, the deaf together met.

The bridegroom, led between two lame men, so
In halting pace and measure, laboured slow :
The bride was led by blind-men just behind—
Because you know that love is always blind.
The hedge-priest called for, then they did him
          bring,
Who married them with an old curtain-ring.
No father was there found or could be ever
She was so old that there was none to give her.

With acclamations now of louder joy
Prayed Hymen Priapus to send a boy,
To shew a miracle ; in vows most deep
The parish swore their children all to keep.

Then Tom-a-Bedlam wound his horn at best
To call the guests unto the marriage-feast :
Pick'd marrow-bones they had found in the street,
Carrots kicked out of kennels with their feet :
And many other dishes that 'twould cumber,
Any to name them ; more than I can number.
Then came the banquet, that must never fail,
Which the town gave, that's white bread and
          strong ale.

All were so tipsy that they could not go,
And yet would dance and cried for 'music ho !'
Gridirons and tongs with keys they played on too,
And blind men sung, as Homer used to do.
Some whistled then and hollow sticks did sound,
And thus melodiously they played a round.

Lame men and women mingled and advanced,
And so, all limping, jovially they danced :
The deaf men joined, for they could not forbear
When they saw this, although they did not hear,
(Which was their happiness): so to the house
They brought the pair and left them drunk as
      a mouse.

THE PHILOSOPHER'S COMPLAINT.*

I through a cranny there did spy
A grave philosopher all sad,
With a dim taper burning by,
His study was in mourning clad.

---

* The verses marked with an asterisk have been materially altered; others have been omitted. Their clumsy
form made them unpresentable. Yet I could not forbear

  * He sighs and thus laments his state :
    Cursing dame Nature, for 'twas she
    That did allot him such a fate
    To make him of mankind of be.

  * All other animals, their mould,
    Of thousand passions makes them free ;
    They are not subject unto gold
    Which doth corrupt mankind we see.

    The busy merchant plies the main,
    The lawyer pleadeth for his fee ;
    Pious divines for lucre's gain,
    Mechanics,—all still cozeners be.

    With plough-shares farmers wound the earth,
    Look to their cattle, swine and sheep,
    To multiply their seed, corn's birth,
    And all for money which they keep.

---

endeavouring to preserve this odd piece, in which here and there occur phrases and thoughts of a *curiosa felicitas*, and through the whole of which runs a quaint, amusing irony. That couplet alone is worth preserving :

<blockquote>' With cares men break their sweet repose
    Like wheels that wear with turning round.'</blockquote>

The sunburnt dame prevents the day,
As her laborious bees for honey,
Doth milk her kine, and spins away
Her fatal thread of life for money.

Mankind doth on god Pluto call
To serve him still in all their pleasure;
Love here doth little; money all,
For of this world it is the measure.

Beasts do despise this Orient metal,
Each freely grazing fills his maw;
After love's procreating settle
To gentle sleep, sweet Nature's law.

They're not litigious but are mute
False propositions never make,
Nor of unknown things do dispute;
Follies for wise things do not take:

* They use not rhetorick to deceive,
Nor logic to enforce the wrong,
Nor strains of tedious history weave,
In tiresome and distracted song:

Nor study the enamelled sky
Thinking they're governed by each star,
But scorn man's false astrology,
And think themselves just what they are.

Their pride not being so supreme,
Celestial bodies moving thus,
Poor mortals cozened with the dream
To think those lights were made for us!

Nor are they troubled where they run,
What the sun's matter it might be ?
Whether the earth moves or the sun—
And yet they know as well as we! *

Nor do they with grave troubled looks
By studious learning force the day,
Or multiplicity of books
To put them out of truth's right way.

High policies beasts never weave
Or subtle traps they never lay,
With false dissemblings that deceive
Their kind to ruin, nor betray.

---

* The irony of this line is peculiarly happy.

The stranger-valued gems that dress
Our beautious ladies like the day,
A parrot's feathers are no less,
It gossips too, as well as they.

Man's always troubled 'bout his fame,
For glory and ambition hot,
While beasts are constantly the same.
In them those follies enter not.

No hopes of worlds to come, that's higher,
In several sects divisions make
Or fear of everlasting fire,
But quiet sleep and calm awake.

* Man's e'er repining for the past
Hating the present that they see,
Frighted at what's to come at last :
Beasts pleased with what is and must be.

Ease man doth hate and piles his store,
A burthen to himself he is,
Weary of time yet wishing more;
Beasts all these vanities do miss.

Man's troubled head and brain's still swelling
Beyond the power of senses five,

Not capable of those things telling :
Beasts beyond senses do not strive.

Nature's just measure senses are,
And no impossibles desire :
Beasts seek not after things that's far
Or toys or baubles do admire.

Beasts slander not or falsehoods raise :
But full of truth as Nature taught,
They wisely shun dissembling ways,
Following dame Nature as they ought :

To no false gods make sacrifice
Or promise vows to break them; no !
No doctrine teach of pious lies,
Or worship gods they do not know,

Nor envy any that do rise,
Or joyful seem at those that fall,
Or crooked plans gainst others tries :
But love their kind, themselves and all.

Hard labour suffer when they must,
When over-awed they wisely bend,
In only patience then they trust
As misery's and affliction's friend.

They seek not after beauty's blaze,
To tempt their appetites when dull;
But drink the streams that tempests raise,
And grumble not when they are full.

With cares men break their sweet repose
Like wheels that wear with turning round;
With beasts calm thoughts their eyelids close
And in soft sleep all cares are drowned.

No rattles, fairings,* ribbons, strings,
Fiddles, pipes, ministrelsies them move
Or bugle-bracelets or fine rings;
And without Cupid they make love.

O happy beasts! that spend the day
In pleasure with their nearest kin,
And all is lawful in their way,
They live and die without a sin.

      *   *   *   *

---

* Presents given at a fair.
   How pedlars' stalls with glittering toys are laid
   The various 'fairings' of the country maid.
                            Gay's Pastorals.

O vain philosophy! Your laws
Only hard words for matter bring :
Which teach us nought—tell not the cause
Or use or end of any thing.

Why are our learned then so proud,
Thinking to bring us to their bow,
Their ignorance wisdom allowed,
Who know not that they do not know?

Or that beasts breath doth downwards go,
Or that men's souls do upward rise,
No post from that world tells you know,
It puzzled Solomon the wise.

———

Thus he complained, and was annoyed
Our grave philosopher, for's birth ;
Both made to think and be destroyed,
Be lost and turned to colder earth.

I pitied him and his sad case
And wished our vicar would him teach,
And the true power of saving grace
With holy rhetorick would preach.

Her face did seem like to a glory bright
Where gods and goddesses did take delight;
And in her eyes new worlds you there might see,
Loves, flying Cupids there as angels be:
And on her lips Venus enthronèd is
Inviting duller lovers there to kiss:
Winged Mercury upon her tongue did sit
Strewing out flowers of rhetorick and of wit;
Pallas did circle in each temple round,
Each with her wisdom as a laurel crowned;
And in her cheeks sweet flowers for Love's gay
    posies
Where Fates spun threads of lilies and of
    roses:
And every loving smile, seemed as it were
A palace for the Graces to dwell there:
And chaste Diana on her snow-white breast
There leaned her head with purest thoughts to
    rest;
When viewed her neck great Jove turned all to
    wonder,
In love's soft showers melting without thunder;

The lesser gods on her soft hands do lie,
Thinking each vein to be their azure sky ;
Her charming circling arms made Mars to
    cease
All his fierce battles for a love's soft peace ;
She on our world's globe sat triumphing
    high,
Heaved there by Atlas up unto the sky.
And sweet breathed Zephyrus there did blow her
    name
In the great glorious trumpet of good fame.

EMIGRANT'S SONG.

[From ' *The Female Wits,*' a play by the Duchess.]

I.

Capt. Let's go to our new plantation,
        Let's go to our new plantation ;
          And there we do hope
          No fear of a rope,
        Nor hanging in that blessèd nation.

II.

Lieut. Let's go to our new plantation,
        Let's go to our new plantation ;

For here's no regard
Nor soldier's reward
In this most wicked nation.

III.

Col. Let's go to our new plantation,
Let's go to our new plantation;
Each man with his wife
Although 'tis hard life
And poverty is our foundation.

FORTUNE.

She seeks not worth and merit to advance,
Her sceptre which she governs by, is chance,
Then said the prince, 'O Fortune most unkind,
I would thou wert as powerless as blind!'

THE DUKE'S EULOGY OF THE DUCHESS'S POEMS AND FANCIES.[*]

I saw your poems, and then wished them mine;
Reading the richest dressings of each line.

---

[*] If this be irony, it will be admitted to be both gracefully and wittily expressed.

Your new-born, sublime fancies in such store
May make our poets blush and write no more.
Nay, Spencer's ghost will haunt you in the night
And Johnson rise, full fraught with venom's spite:
Fletcher and Beaumont, troubled in their graves,
Look out some deeper and forgotten caves:
And gentle Shakespeare weeping, since he must
At best be buried now in Chaucer's dust.
Thus dark oblivion covers every name
Since you have robbed them of their glorious fame.
Such metaphors, such allegories fit
Your judgment weighing out your fresher wit!
By similizing to the life so like,
Your Fancy's pencil's far beyond Vandyke:
Drawing all things to all things at your pleasure,
Which shews your storehouse is the Muses'
    treasure:
You head th' alembic where the Muses sit
Distilling there the quintessence of wit,
Spirits of fancy, essences so sweet!
In you just numbers walk on velvet feet.
    I thought to praise you: but alas! my way
    To yours is night unto a glorious day.

ALLEGORIES,

ESSAYS AND APHORISMS,

BY

THE DUCHESS OF NEWCASTLE.

ALLEGORIES AND ESSAYS.

THE MARRIAGE OF LIFE AND DEATH.

DEATH went a wooing to Life: but his grim and terrible aspect did so affright Life that she ran away, and would by no means hearken to his suit.

Then Death sent Age and Weakness, as two ambassadors, to present his affection; but Life would not give them audience.

Whereupon Death sent Pain, who had such a persuasive power that he made Life yield to Death's desires. And, after they were agreed, the wedding-day was set and the guests invited.

Life invited the five Senses, and all the Passions and Affections, with Beauty, Pleasure,

Youth, Wit, Prosperity; and also Virtue and the Graces. But Health, Strength, Cordials and Charms, refused to come, which troubled Life much.

But none that Death invited refused to come. They were, Old Father Time, Weakness, Sickness, all sorts of Pains, and the Diseases; besides Sighs, Tears and Groans, Numbness and Paleness.

And when Life and Death met, Death took Life by the hand, and Peace married them. Rest made their bed in the chamber of Oblivion, and there Life lay in the cold arms of Death. Yet Death got numerous issues, and ever since whatsoever is produced from Life dies. Whereas before this marriage there was no such thing as dying, for Death and Life were single. But Life proved not so good a wife as Death a husband: for Death is sober, staid, grave, discreet, patient, dwelling silent and solitary: whereas Life is wild, various, inconstant, and runs about shunning her husband Death's company. But he, as a loving and fond husband, follows her; and when he embraces her she soon produces young lives. But all the offspring of Death and Life are divided: half dwelling with Life and half with Death.

At this wedding Old Father Time, which looked the youngest although he was the oldest in the company, danced the nimblest and best, making several changes in his dances. He trod so gently and moved so smoothly that none could perceive how he did turn and wind and lead about. And being wiser than all the rest, with long experience, he behaved himself so handsomely, insinuated so subtilly, courted so civilly, that he got all the ladies' affections: and being dexterous got favours from every one of them, and some extraordinary ones; for he devirginated Youth, Beauty, Pleasure, Prosperity, and all the five Senses; but could not corrupt Wit, Virtue, nor the Graces.

But Nature hearing of the abuse of her Maids was very angry and forced him to marry them all. But they, although they were enamoured of him before they were married, yet now they do, as most other wives, not care for him: nay, they hate him, rail and exclaim against him: that,

what with his peevish, frowned and cross wives
and with the jealousy he hath of Sickness, Pains
and Mischances, which often ravage him, he is
become full of wrinkles and his hair all turned
grey.

But Virtue and Wit are his sworn friends and
sweet companions, and he recreates himself with
their pleasant, free, honest and honourable
societies.

A DISPUTE.

The Soul caused Reason and Love to dispute
with the Senses and Appetites.

Reason brought Religion: for whatsoever
Reason could not make good, Faith did.

Love brought Will: for whatsoever Love said,
Will confirmed.

The Senses brought Pleasure and Pain, which
were as two witnesses. Pleasure was a false
witness: but Pain would not, nor could not be
bribed.

Appetite brought Opinion: which in some
things would be obstinate, in others very facile.

But they had not disputed long, before they were so entangled in their arguments and so invective in their words as most disputers are, that they began to quarrel, as most disputers do.

Whereupon the Soul dismissed them, although with much difficulty: for disputers are captains or colonels of ragged regiments of arguments, and when a multitude are gathered together in a rout they seldom disperse until some mischief is done.

THE MIND AND THE DOCTORS.

The Mind was very sick, and sent for Physicians. Whereupon there came some Divines, but they disputed so long, and contradicted one another so much, that they could conclude nothing. One advised Mind to take a scruple of Calvin's Institutes: others, a drachm of Luther's doctrine: some, two drachms of Romish treacle: some to try Anabaptists' water. Others would have him bound round the head with the Talmud.

But Mind grew sicker and sicker, insomuch that he was almost at his last gasp: whereupon he desired them to depart, 'For,' said he, 'your controversies will kill me before your doctrine will cure me.'

But being very sick, the Mind then sent for other Physicians, who were Moral Philosophers. So, when they were come, they sat round a table, and began to discourse and dispute of the diseases of Mind,

Says one: 'Grief is a lethargy.'

'No,' says another, 'stupidity is a lethargy; for grief rather weeps than sleeps."

'O,—but,' said another, 'there are dry griefs that sweat no tears."

'Pray, gentlemen, dispatch!' said Mind, 'for I'm in great pain.'

Says one: 'Hate is an apoplexy.'

'No,' says another, 'love is an apoplexy: for it is dead to itself, though it lives to another.'

They disputed so long on this point, they had almost fallen out. But the Mind prayed them not to quarrel, for a wrangling noise disturbed him much.

Then one said, 'Spite and envy are cancers; the one caused by sharp humours, the other by salt.'

Another said, that 'Spite was not a cancer, but a fistula, that broke out in many places; and envy was a scurvy that speckled the whole body of the Mind.'

But the Mind prayed them to go no further in that dispute.

Then another said, 'That doubt and hope were an ague in the Mind—doubt being the cold fit and hope the hot.'

A second said, 'That jealousy was an ague.'

'Nay,' said a third, 'jealousy is an hectic fever, which inflames the spirit of action, drinks up the blood of tranquillity, and at last wastes and consumes the body of love.'

And they disputed so much, that they fell together by the ears.

And the Mind was well content to let them fight, but his friends parted them, and prayed the doctors to prescribe the Mind something to take. Then they began their prescriptions.

'For the lethargy of grief,' said the first, 'take some crumbs of comfort, mixed with the juice of patience, the spirits of grace, and the sprigs of time, and lay it to the heart; it will prove a perfect cure.'

Said the second: 'A lethargy is stupidity: and therefore you must take hot and reviving drinks, as wine, variety of objects, and pleasing conversation.'

The one that said envy was a scurvy, bid him 'bathe in solitariness and drink of the water of meditation, wherein run thoughts of death like mineral veins, and it would cure him.' And so they all prescribed according to their own notions of the diseases.

But the Mind perceiving that they agreed not in any one disease or medicine, desired that they would depart from him.

'For,' said he, 'gentlemen, it is impossible you should prescribe an effectual remedy, since you cannot agree about the disease.' So he paid them their fees, and they departed. And the Mind became his own physician, apothecary and surgeon.

First, he let himself blood, opening the wilful vein and taking out the obstinate blood.

Then he took pills made of society and mirth,

and those purged out all strange and vain conceits.

He ate every morning a mess of broth wherein were herbs of grace, gathered from the fields of Scripture, balm of prayer, fruits of justice and kindness, spice of prudence, with bread of fortitude and the water of temperance. This breakfast was a sovereign remedy against the malignant passions, for it tempered the heat, qualified the acridness, and mollifièd the obdurate passions and foolish affections.

Likewise he did take into his service the strongest, soundest and quickest senses: these waited on him, and gave him intelligence of everything: and brought him all the news in the country, which was a recreation and a pastime for him. And by thus doing, he became the healthfullest and jolliest man in the parish.

BODY, MIND, AND TIME.

Body, Mind and Time, had a dispute for preeminency; which dispute was begun by Time. Said he: 'If it were not for me, the

Body would neither have growth nor strength, nor the Mind knowledge nor understanding.'

The Mind answered: 'That though the Body had a fixed time to arrive to a perfect growth, and a mature strength, yet the Mind had not. For I,' said the Mind, 'can never know and understand so much but I might know and understand more. Neither hath Time such tyrannical power over the Mind to bring it to ruin as it hath over the Body.'

'Why,' said the Body, 'Time hath not an absolute power over me either: for Chance and Evil Accidents prevent Time's ruins: and Sickness and ill Diets obstruct and hinder Time's buildings. Neither is it Time that giveth the Mind knowledge and understanding, but the Senses, which are the porters that carry them in and furnish the Mind therewith: without which the Mind would be as empty as a poor thatched house with bare walls, did not the Senses furnish it——'

'And I add to it,' says Time.

But the Mind answered, 'Time is only a lacquey which brings messages, runs errands and presents necessaries for the Mind's use. And had Time no employment, or the Senses no goods to bring in, yet the Mind would not be like a thatched house, empty and unfurnished, for Reason and Judgment, and Imagination would dwell therein, and furnish her with delights. They would make passages of Memory to let objects in, and doors of Forgetfulness to shut them out, and windows of Hope to let in the light of Joy, and shutters of Faith to keep out the chills of Doubt: and long galleries of Contemplation carved and wrought by Imagination, and hung with the pictures of Fancy.'

But, while they were disputing, in comes Death, whose terrible aspect did so affright the Mind, that the very fear put out the light therein, and quenched the flame thereof. And the Body being struck by Death, became senseless and dissolved into dust. But Old Father Time ran away from Death as nimbly as a light-heeled boy, or those that slide upon the ice; and never turned to see whether Death was after him or no.

A QUAINT FANCY.

[From ' *Nature's Pictures drawn by Fancies Pencil.*']

There was a handsome young Lord and a young beautiful Lady, that did love so most passionately and entirely, that their affections could never be dissolved : but their parents not agreeing, would by no means be persuaded to let them marry, nor so much as converse, setting spies to watch them.

But when they found they would meet in despite of their spies, they inclosed them up from coming at each other : whereat they grew so discontent and melancholy, that they both died, just at one and the same time, to the great grief and repentance of their parents who now wished they had not been so cruel.

But when their bodies were dead, these lovers' souls, leaving their fleshly mansions, went towards the river Styx to pass over into the Elysian fields, where on the way they met each other. At which meeting they were extremely joyful, but knew not how to express it, for they had no lips to kiss, nor arms to embrace, being bodiless and only spirits. But the passion of love being always ingenious, found out a way, thus. Their souls did mingle and intermix as liquid essences, whereby their souls became as one. But after some gentle smooth soft love expressions they began to remember each other of their crosses and interpositions whilst they lived in their bodies, at last considering of the place where they were moving to: whither the masculine soul was unwilling to go, for since he had his Beloved he cared not to live in Elysium. Then speaking in the soul's language, he persuaded his love not to go thither, for said he:

'I desire no other company but yours, nor would I be troubled or disturbed with other lovers' souls. Besides, I have heard,' said he, 'they that are there do nothing but walk and talk of their past life; which we may desire to forget. Then let us only enjoy ourselves by intermingling thus.'

She answered she did approve of his desire, and that her mind did join in all consents.

'But where,' said she, 'shall be our habitation ?' *

*　　　*　　　*　　　*　　　*

CHILD LANGUAGE.

Children should be taught at first the best, plainest and purest language, and the most significant words. Not, as their nurses teach them, a strange kind of gibberish—broken languages of their own making—words hashed, mixed, and minced. As, for example, when nurses teach children to go: instead of saying *go*, they say *do, do:* and instead of saying *Come to me*, they say *tum to me :* and when they newly come out of a sleep, and cannot well open their eyes, they do not say *My child cannot well open his eyes*, but

---

* The Duchess having written this charming opening, takes a nonsensical ramble through the stars ; but it appears to me, that for its suggestive quaintness and beauty the fragment is well worth preserving. How finely might the authoress have worked out of discrepancies between the intermingled souls a romance of the most pure and delicate fancy, ray of the highest moral effect ! Is there no living poet to whom this fragment may suggest a poem ?

My child tant open its nies : and when they should bid them *speak*, they bid them *peak;* so all the rest of the language they teach children is after this manner.   When it is as easy for those that teach children, to speak—and more easy for the children to learn to speak—plainly, than this foreign language, which serves them to no use, and afterward only takes up so much more time to learn to speak properly ; time employed in the understanding of sense, which is lost in words.   And it is not only foolish and ill-bred nurses who speak to children thus, but their fathers, who are often accounted wise men, and their mothers, who are often discreet women.   Methinks it is very strange that wise and rational men, when they talk to children, should not strive to make children speak like wise men.   Yet such is the power of custom that wise men follow it, although it be unnecessary, uneasy and foolishly hurtful. For certainly this broken, compounded and false language they teach children, is often so imprinted on the brains, as it can hardly be rubbed out again ; and the tongue gets such a habit of an ill and false pronunciation as, when they are grown to men's and women's estate, their speech flows not so easy or sweet as otherwise it would. And so sometimes they are taught the rudest language first; as, to say *such a one lies*, or to call *Rogues* and the like names, and then laugh as if it were a witty jest!

MISERS.

A prodigal is more beneficial and profitable to the Commonwealth than a usurer; for a prodigal only makes himself poor, whereas a miserable * man makes himself rich and the Commonwealth poor. 'Tis true riches are accounted a great blessing and surely they are so; but I take riches to be only a blessing in the use and not barely in the possession. For riches is not what we have but what we enjoy: for he that hath delicious fruits and will eat sour crabs— hath reviving wines and will drink insipid water— hath stately houses and will live in a thatched cottage—hath stores of fuel and will freeze with cold—and hath great sums of money but will

---

* Miser-able : i.e. miserly.

spend none—he is poorer than they that have but a little and will spend according to their estate. Yet these miserable* men that live starvingly, slovenly and unwholesomely are commended by the moralists and accounted wise men, as not taking pleasure in that they call vanities, which is to make use of their riches, so as to live plentifully, pleasantly, gloriously and magnificently, pleasing themselves with what good fortune hath given them. I for my part had rather live rich and die poor, than die rich and live poor and leave my wealth to those that will be as far from acknowledging my gift with thanks, as it is likely they would rail on my memory, so that my wealth would only build me a tomb of reproaches and a monument of infamy, which would be a just judgment for being so unnatural to myself. Miserable * men believe they are masters to their wealth, because they have it in keeping : whereas they are slaves, not daring to use it unless it be in getting ten in the hundred. But to conclude, those that are miserable* horders

---

* See previous note.

or unconscionable usurers are like weasels or such-like vermin; for as these suck out the meat of an egg so they suck out silver and gold, and leave the Commonwealth like an empty eggshell, which is a penniless purse or treasury.

MARRIAGE.

Those marriages are commonly more happy which are made out of interest than those that are made from fancy. For interest is like brass which is engraven; and fancy is like printed wax. The first never alters, except it be broke by ill fortune; while the other is destroyed by a warm breath.

MEN OUGHT NOT TO STRIVE FOR PRE-EMINENCE WITH WOMEN.

He is either a fool or a coward, that strives for the preeminency with a woman—a coward because he domineers over weakness, a fool to dispute with ignorance. For men should use women as nurses do children, strive to please and yield to them in all things but what will do them harm. As not to suffer them to degrade

themselves of their honours, or spend their estate
by their vanity; or destroy their health by their
ill orders; but to strive to delight them—giving
them liberty in all honourable and honest recreations, in moderate expenses and harmless
vanities. But he that strives with his wife to
win the breeches, would never have had the wit
to have fought the battles of *Cæsar*. For a
gallant man will never strive for the breeches
with his wife, but will present her with the whole
suit, doublet, breeches, and cloak and all appur-
tenances thereto, and leave himself only his
sword to protect her. It is more honour for a
man to be led captive by a woman, than to
contend by resistance. A gallant man willingly
yields to effeminate bands, and takes them rather
as wreaths of flowers than chains of slavery.

WHAT NATURES BAR FRIENDSHIP, AND WHAT MAKE IT.

There are few men that can be true friends.
A cautious man, a politician, a casuist, a jealous
and an amorous man, a choleric and exceptious,

a facile, a false, an envious, a revengeful, a coward, cannot be a true friend; for all their humours turn the bias of friendship another way. A friend must be a wise, honest, valiant, generous, constant, sweet and patient man. But these virtues seldom meet in one person—which makes so many professions and so few performances in friendships. Most people think they could be perfect friends; although there is nothing harder to perform. True friendships are neither confirmed nor known but in extremities, and those extremities seldom come; which makes friendships like bonds that are unsealed. Neither can a man so truly know himself, much less another, as to be assured of having a true and constant friend, except by being one himself. A man may be a friend a thousand years, and in as many extremities (if it were possible), and yet one minute may alter him. So various and inconstant are the passions and affections of men! So little do they know themselves, as not only to be willing at one time to die, but to endure all the torments that life can bear; and again at some other

time they are so fearful as to be willing to part
from that which is most dear for hope of life or
ease from pain. And other accidents, of less
consequence than life, may cross friendship.
Which makes an impossibility of [real] friendship in this world, unless a man have an absolute power over himself, or an unalterable nature
—things that can be only in the society of
angels. But those that may be accounted friends
amongst mankind, are they that do timely cour-
tesies; and to choose friends otherwise is out
of a foolish and affected humour. For one
cannot say, I will choose me a friend for conversation only. That is no friend, who is but a
companion. So an acquaintance, and a companion, and a friend, are several: for I may
have an acquaintance with one, and he not my
companion; and he may be my companion, and
not my friend. But a friend makes the triangle.

WHAT DISCOURSES ARE ENEMIES TO SOCIETY.

Of all discourses, the worst enemy to society
is the divulging the infirmities of others. Some

are so illnatured in striving to defame others, as
that they will not only use their rhetorick to make
faults appear more odious, but will strive to
make virtues seem vices.   To discover infirmities is ignoble, and to lessen virtues the part of
an envious man, and of the nature of a devil.
And since union is the bond of society, the discourse should always tend to peace, and not to
discord.   There is no man but hath virtues to
praise as well as vices to dispraise; and it is as
easy to take the better side.

Another enemy to society is forswearing and
blasphemy.   What pleasure and advantage can
a man have to blaspheme God, who hath power
to return his curses on his head with horrid
punishments?   It shews little wit, and less memory, that men should want words to fill up
their discourse with, but what oaths are fain to
supply.   And for lying—where there is no truth
there can be no trust; and where there is no
trust there can be no union; and where there is
no union there can be no perfect society, but
what may be called a concourse, which is to
meet rather than to unite: while society is the

father of peace, the bond of love, the arm of
strength, the head of policy, the heart of courage,
the hand of industry, and the bowels of charity.
And discourse is the life which gives light to the
eyes of the understanding, sound to the ears,
mirth to the heart, comfort to sorrow and affliction, patience to the oppressed; entertains the
time, recreates the mind, refreshes the memory,
makes the desires known, and is a heavenly
concert.

ADVICE TO PREACHERS.

[Spoken by a Character.]

The preachers for Heaven ought not to
preach factions, nor to show their learning, nor
to express their wit but to teach their flock to
pray rightly; for hard it is to know, whether we
pray or prate; since none can tell the purity of
their own heart or number the follies thereof or
cleanse out the muddy passions that by nature
are bred therein or root out the vices the world
has sown thereon. For if we do not leave out
the world, the flesh and the devil, in our

petitions, and desires we offer to Heaven, it may be said, we rather talk than pray. It is not bended knees or a sad countenance, that can make our prayers authentical or effectual; nor words, nor groans, nor sighs, nor tears, that can pierce Heaven; but a zealous flame raised from a holy fire kindled by a spark of grace in a devout heart, which fills the soul with admiration and astonishment at Jehovah's incomprehensible deity. For nothing can enter Heaven but purity and truth; all the gross and drossy parts fall back with greater force upon our lives and instead of blessings prove curses to us. And the ignorant not conceiving the difference may be lost for want of instruction therein, being most commonly taught the varieties of opinions, the sayings and sentences of the Fathers of the Church, or being exclaimed against for natural imperfections, or threatened for slight vanities. Many, by giving warning against vices, raise those that have been dead and buried with former ages, unaccustomed and utterly unknown to the present auditory. But one good prayer that is directly sent to Heaven buries a multitude

of errors and imperfections, and blots out many
a sin. I speak not this to tax any one here;
for I believe you are all holy men, and reverend
and grave Fathers of the Church, who are
blessed messengers and eloquent orators for
Heaven, the true guides to souls and the example
of a good life.

Then they asked, how they ought to pray?
Whereupon in a zealous passion thus she said—

O God! O God! mankind is much to blame;
He commits faults when he but names His
    name:
His name? saith she, nay deity hath none!
His works sufficient are to make him known,
His wondrous glory is so great, how dare
Man similize? but to Himself compare.
Or how durst men their tongues or lips to
    move
In argument, His mighty power to prove?
As if men's words his power could circle in,
Or trace his ways from whence he did begin,
His mighty works to make, or to what end;
As proudly placing man to be his friend!

Yet poor, proud, ignorant man knows not the
     cause
Of any creature made, much less His laws:
Man's knowledge 's so obscure, not so much
     light
As to perceive the glimmering of His might!
Strive not this deity to comprehend;
He no beginning had, nor can have end:
Nor can mankind His will or pleasure know,
We may not draw Him to expression low.
Let words desist, let's strive our souls to raise;
Let our astonishment be glory's praise:
Let trembling thoughts of fear, as prayers be sent,
And not light words which are by men invent:
Let tongues be silent, adoration pray;
And love and justice lead us the right way.

HONESTY.

There are two sorts of honesty, the one a
bastard the other true born. The bastard is
honest for by-respects; as out of fear of punish-
ment either to reputation, estate or person, or
for love of the reward which honesty brings. But

the true-born honesty loves honesty for honesty's
sake, and is a circle that hath no ends, and
justice is the centre; and honesty is the sweet
essence of nature and a god of humanity.

OF EATING AND DRINKING.

Wine, though it begins like a friend, goes on
like a fool, and most commonly ends, like a
devil, in a fury; yet it is a greater fault to eat too
much than to drink too much wine, in that a
man may live without wine, but not without
meat. For wine is rather a superfluity or curi-
osity than a necessity; but food is the life, and the
staff to support life: and this staff being broken
by excess, famine and plagues ensue, which are
able to destroy a kingdom; while wine may only
destroy some part, but not endanger the whole.
Unless it be every man's particular kingdom,
which is himself, and then indeed it drowns both
king and state.

A MAN SHOULD BE HONEST TO HIMSELF.

Many think that honesty is bound only to
the regard of others and not to themselves. So

indeed an honest man should be a friend and neighbour to all misfortunes, miseries and necessities; helping with kind, loving, and industrious actions in men's distresses, if he think he can assuage them, and do himself no wrong. For every man ought to be honest to himself as well as another. For though we are apt to consider ourselves so much as it may be a prejudice to another, yet we ought not to consider another so much as to be a prejudice to ourselves. For justice to ourselves should take the first place by nature, where to wrong one's self is the greatest injustice.*

FLATTERY.

Flattery takes most when it comes into the ear like soft sweet music, which lulls reason asleep, and enchants the spirits. But if it come in like the sound of a trumpet, it awakes the reason and affrights the mind, and makes it stand upon the guard of defence.

---

* The wise man only will know how to give to these sentiments their proper limitation.

DIVINITY AND MORAL PHILOSOPHY.

Divinity and moral philosophy are the two guardians of nature: yet sometimes they prove two gaolers, when they press or tie their claims too hard.

COURTESY.

Nothing wins more upon the soul of men than civility and courteous behaviour. It endears more than words. For eloquent oratory, though it insinuates, yet is like a tyrant that carries the opinions of men captive by force rather than wins them by gentle persuasion. But a free and civil behaviour causeth affection to run after it—it abates the pride of the proud to meet it—it engentles the wild and barbarous —it softens the rigid—it begets compassion in the cruel—it moves pity in misery—it excites love in prosperity. Most commonly good-nature hath civil and courteous behaviour; but the civil and courteous have not always good natures: so that it becomes verity in the one and hypocrisy in the other; which nevertheless pleaseth, though it be a fair face to a false heart.

YOUTH.

Youth ought to have good and grave counsels and solid studies to poise it. For if the bottom or keel of life be not balanced, the sails of vanity will overturn the ship of happiness. For it is not those light counsels that parents do vulgarly use to give their children that make them wise; as saying 'Take heed of catching cold,—or not eating such and such meats,' or teaching them how to put off their hat, or make a leg with a good grace, though that doth well. Nor yet is it keeping them too hard to their studies, for that makes them most commonly pedantic. But send them abroad to learn to know the world, that they may see men and manners and observe natures, customs, laws and ceremonies. The knowledge of the world gives a satisfaction to the mind: for when they see there is change, and that misfortunes are not to be avoided, they will not make every little cross an affliction, but take afflictions as things necessary and to be borne with patience. And so they shall live more happily and die more willingly.

OF GENTLEWOMEN THAT ARE SENT TO BOARDING SCHOOLS.

It is dangerous to put young women to boarding schools, unless their parents live so disorderly that their children may grow wicked or base by their examples. For most commonly in these schools they learn more vices than manners. It is a good task for one body to bring up one child well, and, as they ought to be bred, at most two or three; but it is too much for one to breed up many — as for one woman to breed up twenty young maids. It is true they may educate their persons, but it is a doubt whether they do or can educate their minds. They may teach them to sing well, but it is a question whether they teach them to think well. They may teach them measures with the feet, and yet to mistake the measures of a good life. They may teach them to write by rule, but forget the rules of modesty.

For the danger is in those schools where there are a great many gentlewomen of several families and births, degrees of ages, various humours, different dispositions, natures and qualities, that they do, like several sorts of fruits, which, when they are gathered and heaped together, soon putrify and corrupt, and some become rotten at the core. Whereas, if every pear, apple, and plum, were laid by themselves apart in a dry and clean place, they would be found wholesome, and last as long as it was their nature to last. So if young women were bred singly, carefully and industriously, one by one, there would be no danger of their learning from each other craft, dissembling, fraud, spite, slander, and the like. Besides, where there are many together of several dispositions, they are not only apt to catch the infection of ill qualities from each other, but often breed vices, which ruin themselves, their fortunes and families, and, like maggots, consume their estates or eat a hole in their reputation.

Besides, all board scholars of the effeminate sex are like sale-meat dressed at a cook's shop, which always tastes of the dripping-pan or smoke. So most commonly those that are bred at schools have a smack of the school, at least in their behaviour—that is, constraint: And their exercises, though they are commendable in women of quality, yet it is not these exercises or *virtues* (as they call them in *Italy*) which give them good breeding, but to instruct their youth in useful knowledge, to correct their ignorance with right understanding, to settle their minds to virtue, to govern their passions by reason, to rule their insatiable or distempered appetites with temperance; to teach them noble principles, honourable actions, modest behaviours, civil demeanours,—to be cleanly, patient and pious; things which none can teach either by example or instruction, or both, but those that have been nobly bred themselves.

THE ANT AND THE BEE.

(A FABLE.)

It chanced that an ant and a bee, wandering about, met in a honey-pot; the honey being very clammy stuck so close to the ant and weighed so heavy that she could not get out, but (like a horse in a quagmire) the more pains she took to get out, the deeper she sunk in; whereupon she entreated the bee to help her.

The bee denied her, saying she should become guilty of theft in assisting a thief.

' Why,' said the ant, ' I do not entreat you to assist my stealth, but my life; but for all your pretended honesty and nicety of conscience, you endeavour to steal honey as much as I.'

' No,' said the bee, ' this honey was stolen by men out of our commonwealth; and it is lawful not only to challenge our own, but to take it wheresoever we find it; besides man (most commonly) doth cruelly murder us by smothering us with smoke, then destroy our city and carry away the spoils.'

The ant said, ' I hope that the cruelty you condemn and have found by experience in man, will cause you to be so charitable as to help me out of my misery.'

' There is no reason in that,' answered the bee; ' for if man doth unjustly strive to destroy me, it doth not follow I must unjustly strive to help you.'

Now, whilst the bee was thus talking, the honey had clammed her wings close to her sides so that she could not loosen them to fly, and in struggling to get liberty for flight plunged her whole body in the honey.

'O,' said the bee, 'I shall be swallowed up and choked immediately!'

'What,' said the ant, 'with your own honey?'

'O,' said the bee, 'the quantity devours me, for water refreshes life and drowns life; meat feeds the body and destroys the body by surfeits: a creature may choke with that which might nourish it.. O unhappy creature that I am,' said the bee 'that my labour and industry should prove my ruin!'

But the honey rising above her head stopped her speech and killed her. The ant after a short languishing died also. Thus we see the same mercy and assistance we refused to others, is refused to us in the like distress, and many times in the midst of abundance are our lives taken away. When we are too greedily earnest

in keeping or taking what we can justly call
our own we seldom enjoy it, either through
losing it or ourselves.*

WIT.

Wit cheers the heart, refreshes the spirits,
delights the mind, entertains the thoughts,
sweetens melancholy, dresses joy, mourns with
sorrow, pleaseth lovers, excuseth falsehoods,
mends faults, begs pardon. Wit is a fine companion, either in private closets, full courts, or
on long travels. Wit is neither troublesome nor
changeable. Wit hath no bottom, but is like a
perpetual spring. Wit is the sun of the brain.

FOOLS.

The *self-conceited fool* is one that scorns to
take counsel, and not only thinks his fancy the
fullest of wit, and his judgment the wisest, and
his actions the regularest, but that *his* house, *his*

---

* The Authoress here but imperfectly points the moral
of her own fable, not the least telling part of which is the
bee's casuistry.

horse, *his* dog, *his* anything is best. Not for the conveniences of his house, or for its beautiful architecture or situation; or that his· horse is the strongest, soundest, best-natured, choicest-coloured, fullest of spirit, swiftest of race, surest of foot; or that his dog is the best hound to hunt withal, or the best spaniel to couch withal, or the best greyhound to run withal, or the best mastiff to fight withal: it is not for the worth or benefit which he receives from anything that he loves or esteems it; but he thinks that whatsoever is good, pleasant, or profitable, is created so by being His.

The *impatient fool* is all for the present: for he thinks his throat cut until he be satisfied in his desires. A day to him is as a thousand years. And he scarce thinks of heaven because he enjoys it not.

The *learned fool* admires and is in love with all other languages besides his own, for if he were bred with the Greek or Hebrew, which are accounted the most significant, he would prefer Low Dutch, which hath the least compass, before it. He is proud of being acquainted with several authors, although his acquaintance oppresseth his memory, smothers his judgment by the multitude of opinions, kills his health by study, destroys his natural wit by the transplantings and engraftings of what he reads. Then he is so bound up to rules as to give himself no reasonable liberty.

The *superstitious fool* is an observer of times, postures, figures, noises, accidents and dreams. As for times—he will not begin a journey, or marry, or buy land, or build, or begin any work, but on such days as are lucky. For dreams— if he dreams that his teeth fall out of his head, or of flowers, or gardens, or anything green, or to see his face in a glass, or to fall from a precipice, or be at weddings, he thinks it fatal. For noises—the howling of dogs, the croaking of ravens, the singing of crickets, the screeching of owls. For accidents—the bleeding that drops at the nose, the right eye itching, salt falling to him. For postures or figures—a hare to run across him, or a stumble at the door. Insomuch as he never enjoys any present recreation, for fear of an evil accident.

The *venturous fool* thinks all desperate actions honourable valour; as to go into the field of battle unarmed, or to wear something as a mark for the enemy to shoot at, or to give the enemy any advantage; where the honour of the valiant is to beat, and not to be beaten: for he is a fool that will give his enemy ground. And others think it a valour to leap over hedges and ditches and gates, to swim or make their horses swim over large and deep rivers, or to try experiments upon themselves; and all to no purpose but to shew what they dare do. Whereas true valour will do none of these actions, unless it be upon strong necessities. These fools run blindfold into actions; and as the proverb saith, *They leap before they look*, and stumble at straws. But as fools make all things worse than they are in not giving them the right use, so wise men prevent evils by their foresight, mend what is bad, shun danger, and what cannot be avoided they bear with patience.

The *busy fool* is one that had rather break his head at his neighbour's door than keep it whole at home. He is the hackney for news, loading himself at the post-house and disburdening himself to all he meets. He is more concerned with a foreign ambassador, though he hath no use of him, than the ambassador is with his embassies. He never faileth sessions, assizes, and executions. He riseth early, eats hastily, walks fast, goeth to bed late, and his thoughts beat quicker than a feverish pulse. He is full of vain designs ; offers his services to all, though he is not able to do any; strives to know all things, and takes no time to learn anything. He makes himself his greatest enemy.

The *captious fool* is one that thinks that all which is said is meant against him. He hates whispering or laughing in any besides himself, and is jealous of all men. He is as a troubled water, where no beast will drink.

The *prodigal fool* is like a weak stomach, that whatsoever it receives it casts forth. Which makes his purse like his body, to die of a consumption.

I have heard say, that *The world is as one great fool ;* and in the world, say some, *The wise, though there be very few, are buried in the rubbish of fools without monuments.*

PERSONATION OF WRITINGS.

Writings are of several and different natures. Some are magistrates that endeavour to reprove and reclaim men—as moral philosophers. Others are attorneys to inform them—as historians. Some are lawyers, to plead in behalf of former writings, and take action against others —as controversialists. Some are ambitious tyrants, who would kill all who stand in their way —as critics. Some are scouts—as natural philosophers. (But they bring not always true intelligence.) Some are hangmen—as sceptics, who strive to strangle not only all opinions, but all knowledge. Some are ambassadors, sent to condole and congratulate — as homilists and psalmists. Some are merchants, as translators, which traffic out of one language into another. Some are conjurors, that fight with their threatening prophecies. Some are cut-purses, that steal from the writings of others. Some are mountebanks, that deceive and give more words than matter. Some are buffoons, that laugh and jest at all. Some are like God, who is full of truth, and gives the due to all deceivers. Some are devils, that slander and injure all alike.

MAN'S PREEMINENCE.

Some say a man is a nobler creature than a woman, because our Saviour took upon Him the body of a man: and others, that man was made first. But these two reasons are weak. For the Holy Spirit took upon Him the shape of a dove, which creature is of less esteem than mankind: and for the preeminency in creation, the devil was made before man.

A DAUGHTER'S DYING SPEECH TO HER FATHER.

Father, farewell! And may that life which issues from my young and tender years, be added to your age! May all your grief be buried in my grave; and may the joys, pleasures, and delights, that did attend my life, be servants unto yours! May comfort dry your eyes, God cease your sorrows, that though I die, you may live happily. Why do you mourn that death must be your son-in-law? since he is a better husband than any you could choose me or I could choose myself. It is a match that Nature and the Fates have made; wherefore be content, for destiny cannot be opposed. But, if you could, you would rob me of the happiness that God intends me. For though my body shall dwell with death, my soul shall dwell in heaven; and holy angels that are my marriage guests, will conduct it to that glory for which you have cause to joy, and not to grieve; for all creatures live but to die, but those that are blessed die to live: and so do I. Farewell.

A BARRISTER'S FUNERAL ORATION.

Dear Friends—You see the body of Serjeant N. lies dead, ready to be put into the grave, which shews that he would not plead for life, or else Death had no ears to hear his suit. But if he pleads as well for himself at God's tribunal as he did for his clients at the bar, he will get judgment on his side. Nature as well as education made him a pleader, for naturally he had a flowing speech and a fluent wit to turn, wind and form any cause as he liked best. And had he not known the laws as well as he did, his wit and eloquence would have covered his ignorance and supplied the defect of his learning. But he was as good and learned a lawyer, as an excellent pleader, and as honest a man as either, for he took more pains to plead his clients' causes than pleasure in taking his clients' fees. Neither would he prolong his clients' suits to drain their purses. He pleaded gratis for his poor clients. He not only took pains for his clients, but pleasure in his own wit; and not so much pleasure in those as others did which heard him. He reproached no man, nor used railing speeches nor violent actions in his argument, as many, nay most pleaders, do; but his behaviour was civil, his wit sweet, and his speech gentle. Though his wit was quick, ready, and free, it was neither salt, sour, nor bitter. Though his speech was flowing, it was not rough—it ran in a smooth though full stream, and his demeanour was so graceful and becoming, that the one delighted the eyes of the beholders as much as the other the ears of the hearers. But though his body be dead his wit, eloquence, elegance, honesty and abilities are living in the memory of living men, and will live, by tradition, so long as there are men to remember and speak. Wherefore let us keep his living parts in our minds, and bury his dead parts in the grave,—the one to remain in Peace, the other in Fame.

A POST-RIDER'S FUNERAL.

This man did not think, when he got on the horse's back, he should ride post to death; for had he thought so, he would have chosen to run a-foot, a safer though a slower pace. But could his soul ride post on death to heaven, as his body rid post on a horse to death, he might outstrip many a soul that is gone before him, &c.

A CHILD'S FUNERAL ORATION.

Beloved Brethren,—We are the funeral guests to a young child, an infant, who died soon after it was born; and though all men are born to live and live to die, yet this child was born to die before it had lived—I mean in comparison of the age of men. Thus he was born, cried and died—a happy conclusion for the child, that he had finished what he was made for in so short a time, &c.

THE TOBACCONIST.

There were two maids talking of husbands; for that is for the most part the theme of maids' discourse, and the subject of their thoughts.

Said one to the other: ' I would not marry a man that takes tobacco for anything.'

Said the second : ' Then it is likely you will have a fool for a husband; for though it doth not always work to wise effects, by reason some fools are beyond improvement, it never fails where improvement is to be made.'

'Why,' said the first, 'how doth it work such wise effects?'

'It composes the mind—it busies the thoughts—it attracts all outward objects to the mind's view—it settles and soothes the senses—it clears the understanding—strengthens the judgment—spies out errors—evaporates follies—it heats ambition—it comforts sorrow—it abates passions—it digests conceptions—it elevates imaginations—it creates fancies—it quickens wit.'

Said the first: 'It makes the breath stink.'

WITS.

[From '*The Comical Hash*,' a Play by the Duchess.]

Enter the Lady CENSURER *and the Lady* EXAMINATION.

Ex. Lady *Censurer*, pray, what think you of the Lady *Retort's* wit—hath she not a great wit?

Cens. O fie! She hath a chambermaid's wit.

Ex. What wit is that, Lady?

Cens. Why, a snip-snappy wit.

Ex. Indeed, I have heard many nursery-maids

give so sharp and quick replies, as amongst some they would be judged to be great wits, yet come to discourse seriously with them, and they were not much wiser than beasts. But what do you think of the Lady *Sharp's* wit?

Cens. Her wit fetches the skin off the ears; it corrodes the mind of the hearers more than vinegar the tongues of the tasters.

Ex. How approve you of the Lady *Courtly's* wit?

Cens. Her wit is tedious, as all complimenting wits are; they tire one's ears.

Ex. What think you of the Lady *Learning's* wit?

Cens. Her wit is an alms-tub: it yields nothing but scraps, relics and broken pieces.

Ex. What think you of the Lady *Subtlety's* wit?

Cens. Her wit is lime, twigs, snares and traps, to catch fools with.

Ex. How like you the Lady *Fancy's* wit?

Cens. Her wit indeed is a true natural wit—it is sweet and delightful, easy and pleasing—as being free and unconstrained.

WOMEN'S RIGHTS.

[AN ORATION.]

Noble, honourable and virtuous women—the former oration was to persuade us to change the custom of our sex, which is a strange and unwise persuasion, since we cannot change the nature of our sex. For we cannot make ourselves men and have female bodies, and yet to act masculine parts will be very preposterous and unnatural. In truth we shall make ourselves like as the defects of nature, to be hermaphroditical, as to be neither perfect women nor perfect men, but corrupt and imperfect creatures. Wherefore let me persuade you, since we cannot alter the nature of our persons, not to alter the course of our lives, but to rule our lives and behaviours, so as to be acceptable and pleasing to God and men; which is to be modest, chaste, temperate, humble, patient and pious; also to be housewifely, cleanly and of few words, all which will gain us praise from men, blessing from heaven, love in this world and glory in the next.

APHORISMS.

I

MOST MEN'S minds are insipid, having no balsamical virtue therein; they are as the *Terra
Damnata* of nature.

And their brains are most commonly barren
grounds, which bear nothing but mossy ignorance—no flowers of wit. The courses of their
lives are like those who dig in a coal-pit; their
actions as the coals therein, by which they are
smutched and blacked with infamy. Or else
their actions are like a sexton, who digs a grave
to bury a life in oblivion.

II

THOUGHTS are like stars in the firmament;
some are fixed, others like the wandering planets,
others again are only like meteors. Understanding is like the Sun, which gives light to all the

thoughts. Memory is like the Moon, it hath its new, its full, and its wane.

III

THE WORLD is a shop which sells all manner of commodities to the soul and senses: the prices are good actions and bad; for which they have salvation or damnation: peace or war: pleasure or pain: delight or grief.

IV

THE EARTH is the great merchant of the world,* trafficking with the Sun and the rest of the planets: whose storehouses are the several regions from whence she fetches, in ships of attraction, her several commodities, heat and moisture, whereof she makes life, and sells it to several creatures who pay her death for the same.

---

* *i. e.* Universe.

V

Wit is like a lily, the one is as pleasant to the ear as the other is to the eye. It comes to fading naturally, and if it be not timely gathered, it soon withers and dies.

VI

Prudence is like an oak : it is long a growing and it is old before it dies.

VII

Melancholy is the North pole : Envy the South : Choler is the Torrid zone : and Ambition is the Zodiack : Joy is the Ecliptic line where the Sun of mirth runs : Justice is the Equinoctial : Prudence and Temperance are the Arctic and Antarctic circles : Patience and Fortitude are the Tropics.

VIII

Man is like the globe of the world, and his head as the highest region : wherein knowledge as the sun runs in the ecliptic line of reason, and gives light and understanding to all the rest of the thoughts as stars which move by degrees in their several orbits, some slower and some faster. Ignorance is the total eclipse. The violent passions are as dark clouds that veil the sun's face, which is only seen by its shadows, but not in its full glory.

IX

THE WORLD is a great city, wherein is much commerce; and through which runs a great, navigable river of ambition, ebbing and flowing with hope and doubt. Thereon are floating barks of self-conceit filled with pride and scorn —and merchants of faction set forth ships of trouble to bring in power and authority. And these ships by the storms of war are often wrackt,* where all happiness and peace is drowned in waves of misery and discontent. But silver vows, gilded promises and golden expectations, make a glorious shew in all the streets. And though substance does not waste, yet it is often

* *i. e.* Wrecked.

melted by cross accidents and forgetfulness; and
the fashions alter according to the humours of
the time. Hard hearts, bold faces, seared con-
sciences and rash actions, are the brass and
iron that make the instruments of protection and
offence.

X

Fancies are tossed in the brain as a ball
against a wall, where every bound begets an
echo. So from one fancy arise more.

XI

The brains of men are like colleges, and the
thoughts the students that dwell therein: thus
many heads may make up an university.

XII

Some eyes allure hearts, as falconers do
hawks.

XIII

Falsehoods are like caps which cover the
head of knowledge from the sun of truth: or

like vaults and woods that make echoes, where words spread far and sound double and treble: or like multiplying glasses, which make of one a thousand.

XIV

THERE is no way to clear thoughts but by words.

XV

THEY who take self-love for their guide ride in the ways of Partiality, on the horse of Flattery to the judgment of Falsehood.

XVI

IF a woman gets a spot on her reputation, she can never rub it out.

XVII

SOME give women more praises than their modesty dares countenance.

XVIII

IT IS BETTER TO LIVE

> With Liberty than with Riches.
> With Virtue than with Beauty.
> With Love than with State.
> With Health than with Power.
> With Wit than with Company.
> With Peace than with Fame.
> With Beasts than with Fools.

XIX

THERE is no greater usury or extortion than upon courtesy; for the loan of money is but ten, twenty, or thirty, on the hundred; but the loan of courtesy is to enslave a man all his life.

XX

GOD, by Fortune, does not always protect the honest from the envious, or from the accidents of chance.

XXI

LOVE and POWER are like the sun. When the beams are drawn together in one point, it burns.

XXII

OF all virtues, PATIENCE hath the fewest passions mixed with it: and, though it seems insensible, yet it seeth clearly into its own misfortunes. For Patience belongs only to the misfortunes that concern a man's self. Yet Patience should never be a bawd to a man's ruin.

XXIII

THERE are wings to perfect love; but no body can arrive to the journey's end until they come to heaven.

XXIV

SOME BRAINS are barren grounds, that will not bring seed or fruit forth, unless they are well manured with the old wit which is raked from other writers and speakers.

XXV

OTHERS are like foolish husbandmen, that sow a crop either too soon or too late, which makes their brains unprofitable.

XXVI

OLD MAIDS are most commonly scorned and despised, out of a corrupt nature in mankind which strives to scandalize virtue.

XXVII

PAIN and OBLIVION make mankind afraid to die; but all creatures are afraid of the one, none but mankind afraid of the other.

XXVIII

THERE is no sound strikes so hard as the report of DEATH: especially when affection opens the door and lets the messenger down into the heart.

XXIX

TRUE LOVE is an affection which is very difficult to settle, and hard to remove when once placed.

XXX

SOME PAINTERS are only fit for signposts: some wits for ballads.

XXXI

None gain by quarrels but lawyers, whose fees are begot by discord.

XXXII

Some are so envious, as when they cannot hope to be the highest, they would be content to be miserable to see others so.

XXXIII

It is not every ambitious and aspiring spirit that can do brave and noble actions.

XXXIV

One natural English tongue was significant enough, without the help of other languages; but as we have merchandize for wares so have we done for words—but indeed we have rather brought in than carried out.

XXXV

Prosperity is like perfume, it often makes the head ache.

XXXVI

Translation is a good work: yet translators are but like those that shew the tombs at Westminster or the lions at the Tower, who are but informers, not owners of them.

XXXVII

Although accidents give the ground to some arts, yet they are rude and uneasy until the brain hath polished them over.

XXXVIII

Moralists are like powerful monarchs which can make their passions obedient at their pleasure, condemning them at the bar of justice, cutting off their heads with the sword of reason; or, like skilful musicians, making the passions musical instruments, which they can tune so exactly and play so well and so sweetly, as every several note shall strike the ear of the soul with delight: and when they play concords, the mind dances in measure the saraband of tranquillity.

XXXIX

IMITATIONS are like a flight of wild geese, which go each one after another; while singularity is like a phœnix, having no companion nor competitor, which makes it the more admired.

XL

A WICKED man's heart is like a snake of wire put up round in a box, that when it is opened by base and cruel actions, flies in the face of those who stand by it.

XLI

PLATONIC LOVE is a bawd to adultery.

XLII

A MAN may be as soon dishonoured by the indiscretion of his wife as by her dishonesty.

XLIII

A MAN should always wear his life for the service of his honour.

XLIV

TYRANTS may be said to keep their power by the sweat of their brow.

XLV

TEARS are apt to flow especially from moist brains. But deep sorrow hath dry eyes, silent tongues, and aching hearts.

SELECTIONS

FROM THE

'CCXI LETTERS'

OF THE

DUCHESS OF NEWCASTLE.

'CCXI LETTERS.'

BEAUTY.

MADAM,—The Lady C— ought not to be reproved for grieving for the loss of her beauty; for beauty is the light of our sex, which is eclipsed in middle age and benighted in old age; wherein our sex sits in melancholy darkness and the remembrance of beauty past is as a displeasing dream. The truth is, a young, beautiful face is a friend—whereas an old, withered face, is an enemy. Yet I am not of Mrs. U. R's humour, who had rather die before her beauty, than that her beauty should die before her. For I had rather live with wrinkles, than die with youth: and had rather my face clothed with

Time's sad mourning, than with Death's white hue. And surely it were better to follow the shadow of beauty than that beauty should go with the corpse to the grave : and I believe that Mrs. U. R. would do, as the tale is of a woman, that did wish and pray she might die before her husband, but when Death came, she entreated him to spare her and take her husband : so that she would rather live without him than die for him. But leaving this sad discourse of age, wrinkles, ruin and death,

I rest, Madam,

Your very faithful friend and servant.

THE THREE BEAUTIES.

MADAM,—The other day was here the Lady J. to see me, and her three daughters, who are called the three Graces. The one is black *, the other brown, the third white—all three dif-

---

* The Duchess's fancy has here carried her out of the regions of beauty as well as of probability.

ferent coloured beauties. Also they are of different features, statures and shapes; yet all three so equally handsome, that neither judgment nor reason can prefer one before another. Also their behaviours are different—the one is majesical, the other gay and airy, the third meek, and bashful, yet all three graceful, sweet and becoming. Also their wits are different—the one propounds well, the other argues well, the third resolves well; all which make a harmony in discourse. These three ladies are resolved never to marry, which makes many sad lovers. But whilst they were here, in comes the Lord S. C., and, discoursing with them, at last he asks them, whether they were seriously resolved never to marry? They answered, 'they were resolved never to marry.' 'But, ladies,' said he, 'consider, time wears out youth and fades beauty; and then you will not be the three young, fair Graces.' 'You say true, my Lord,' answered one of them, 'but when we leave to be the young, fair Graces, we shall then be old, wise Sybils.' By this answer you may perceive that when one sex cannot pretend to be fair, they will pretend to be wise.

But it matters not what we pretend to, if we be really virtuous, which I wish all our sex may be.

> And rest, Madam, &c.

A BAD MAN WRITING HIS OWN LIFE.

MADAM,—In your last letter you sent me word 'that Sir F. O. was retired to write his own life, for he says he knows no reason but he may as well write his own life as *Guzman*,' and since you desire my opinion of his intended work, I can only say, that his life, for anything I know to the contrary, hath been as evil as Guzman's. But whether his wit be as good as Guzman's, I know not; yet I doubt the worst. And to write an evil life without wit, will be but a dull and tedious story—indeed so tedious and dull, as I believe none will take the pains to read it, unless he reads it himself. But it is to be hoped that he will be tired of himself, and so desist from his self-story. And if he do write his own life, it will be as a masking dolphin, or such like thing, where the outside is painted pasteboard or canvas, and the inside stuffed with shreds of paper or dirty rags. But if he have any friends, surely they will persuade him to employ his time about something else. Some are so unhappy as to have nothing to employ time with. They can waste time, but not employ time; and as they waste time, so time wastes them. There's a saying, *That men are born to live, and live to die;* but I think some are only born to die, and not to live; for they make small use of life, and life makes small use of them—so that in effect they were ready for the grave as soon as they came forth from the womb. Wherefore, if Sir F. O. go forward with his work, he will dig his grave through the story of his life, and his soul-less wit will be buried therein. But leaving his dead wit to his paper coffin, and his unprofitable labours to his black, mourning ink,

I rest, Madam, &c.

THE AGE.

MADAM,—I am sorry to hear wit is so little known and understood, that Sir W. T. should be thought mad because he hath more wit than other men. Indeed, wit should always converse with wit, and fools with fools: for wit and fool can never agree, they understand not one another. Wit flies beyond a fool's conceit, for wit is like an eagle—it hath a strong wing, and flies high and far, and when it doth descend, it knocks a fool on the head as an eagle doth a dotril * or a woodcock. And surely the world was never so filled with fools as it is in this age, nor have there been greater errors or grosser follies committed than in this age. It is not an age like Augustus Cæsar's, when wisdom reigned and wit flourished. But in this age debauchery is taken for wit and faction for wisdom, treachery for policy, and drunken quarrels for valour. Indeed, the world is so foolishly wicked and basely foolish, that they are happiest who can withdraw themselves most from it. But you say, 'every particular complains of the world,' as I do in this letter, 'yet none helps to mend it.' Let me tell you, Madam, it is not in the power of every

---

* Dotril or dotterel; a silly bird of any species.

particular, nor in a number, but the chiefest
persons must mend the world—viz. they that
govern the world; or else the world will be out
at heels. But in some ages the world is more
tattered and torn than in other ages; and in
some ages the world is patched and pieced, but
seldom with what is new and suitable. And
oftener it is in a fool's coat than in a grave
cassock. Wherefore, leaving the motley,

I rest, Madam, &c.

TIME.

Madam,—I remember you told me that formerly you thought Time troublesome, and every
place wearisome. As, in the spring you would
wish for summer: when summer came you
would wish for autumn: and in autumn you
would wish for winter—a cold wish : nay, every
day, every hour, every minute, you thought
tedious and long. Time, indeed, runs so fast
upon youth, as it doth oppress youth, which
makes youth desire to cast it by. Though the
motion of time is swift, the desire of youth is

R 2

swifter.   So youth, through its sharp, greedy, hungry appetite, devours time, as a cormorant doth fish; for he never stays to chew, but swallows down whole fishes: so youth swallows whole days, weeks, months and years, until surfeited with practice or fully satisfied with experience.   Youth is not satisfied, because it hath not had enough variety of knowledge: they know not the unprofitable use of variety, nor know they the deceits, abuses, and treacheries of their own kind, nor their own natures and dispositions.   They know not what to choose or what to leave—what to seek or what to shun. Neither have they felt the heavy burden of cares, the oppressions of sorrow for losses and crosses; they have not been pinched with necessity, nor pained with long sickness, nor stung with remorse; they have not been terrified with bloody wars, nor forsaken of natural friends, nor betrayed by feigned friendships, nor robbed of all their maintenance, nor banished their country. Thus being tenderly young, they are oppressed with the quick repetitions of time; and their senses being sharp, and their appetites hungry,

they devour time, who in the end devours them
—the meat the eater. The desire of knowledge
makes every place wearisome. For youth takes
delight in that which is new: being new themselves, they sympathetically delight in new things
—new clothes, new houses, new varieties, new
sports, new countries, new companions, new
lovers, new friends and anything that is new,
insomuch as they would rather have a new
enemy than an old friend. And thus they will do
until Time turns his back, whereon are written
all the follies of youth, which follies they could
not see to read while Time was before them ;
for while his face was towards them, they only
saw the childish desires which were all written
upon Time's breast. Time is like a courting
Amoroso, it makes love to all, and then forsakes
all it hath made love to. Madam, it hath but
newly turned its head from you, but it will turn
its whole body. At first it will seem to pace
slowly from you, but it will mend its pace, and
at last run from you. Let it not run without
repining or grieving for its neglects, for no persuasion will make it stay. But, Madam, you

will be happier in Time's neglects than his embraces, and will make more advantage from his heels than from his head—for Time's head is filled with vanity, and on Time's heels is experience. And although Time runs from you, Wisdom will stay with you; for Wisdom is the son of Time, and became wise by his father's follies; which are written on his father's back. Wisdom waits always behind his father, and neither Wisdom the son, nor Time the father, do meet face to face. You will find more happiness in Wisdom's company than in Time's courtships. But lest this letter should be as tedious to you as formerly Time was, I'll stop here. And rest,

Madam, &c.

TALK.

MADAM,—The Lady P. R. was to visit the Lady S. I., and other ladies with her, whose conversation and discourse was according to their female capacities and understandings: and when they were all gone, Lady S. I.'s husband asked his wife, 'Why she did not talk as the rest of the ladies did, especially the Lady P. R., so loudly and impertinently?' She answered, 'She had neither the humour, breath, voice, nor wit, to speak so long, so loud and so much, of nothing.' He said her answer liked him well, for he would not have his wife so bold, so rude and so talking a fool. Thus, Madam, we may perceive how discourse in conversation is judged of, and for the most part condemned by the hearers, when perchance the ladies imagine that they are applauded and commended for their wit and confident behaviour. For self-love thinks all is well said or done that itself speaks or acts. But leaving self-love to self-admiration, and that admiration to others condemnation,

I rest, Madam, &c.

ELOQUENCE.

MADAM,—In your last letter you were pleased to condemn me for admiring words so much as to prefer eloquence before all other music. But pray, Madam, mistake me not; for 1 do not admire the words, but the sense, reason and wit that is expressed and made known by words. Neither do I admire orators that speak premeditated orations, but natural orators who can speak on a sudden upon any subject—whose words are as sweet and melting as manna from heaven, and their wit as spreading and refreshing as the serene air; whose understanding is as clear as the sun, giving light of truth to all their hearers: who in case of persuasion speak sweetly, in case of reproof seasonably, and in all cases effectually. And, Madam, if you do consider well, you cannot choose but admire and wonder at the powers of eloquence, for there is a strange, hidden mystery in it—it hath a magical influence over mankind—it charms the senses and enchants the mind and is of such commanding power as to force the will to rule the actions of the body and soul to do or to suffer beyond their natural abilities—it makes the souls of men the tongue's slaves. Such is the power of an eloquent speech, that it binds the judgment, blindfolds the understanding, and deludes the reason. It softens obdurate

hearts, and causes dry eyes to weep and dries
wet eyes from tears. It refines the drossy humours, polishes rough passions, bridles unruly
appetites, reforms rude manners, and calms troubled minds. It can civilize the life by virtue,
and inspire the soul with devotion. On the
other side, it can enrage the thoughts to madness, and cause the soul to despair. The truth
is, it can make men like gods or devils—having
a power beyond nature, custom and force: for
many times the tongue hath been too strong for
the sword and carried away the victory. Also
it hath been too subtle for the laws, as to banish
right and condemn truth: and too hard for the
natures of men, making their passions its pri-
soners. . . . . Wit makes a ladder of words to
climb to Fame's high tower : and the tongue
carries men further than their feet, and builds
them a statelier and more lasting palace than
their hands—and their wit more than their wealth
doth adorn it. But now, leaving words and wit
I rely upon love and friendship, and rest,

Madam, &c.

A DEFENCE OF HER MANNER OF LIFE.

MADAM,—I heard by your last that the Lady S. P. was to visit you, where amongst her other discourse she spoke of me, and was pleased to censure and condemn—as to censure the cause and condemn the manner of my life, saying that I did either retire out of a fantastic humour, or otherwise I was constrained in not having the liberty that other wives usually have to go abroad and receive what visitors they please. If she did but know the sweet pleasures and harmless delights I have by this retirement, she would not have said what she did. To answer what she said, this course of life is my own voluntary choice, for I have liberty to do anything or to go anywhere, or to keep any company that discretion doth allow and honour approve of: and though I may err in my discretion, I do not in cases of honour, for had I not only liberty, but were persuaded or enticed by all the world's allurements, or were threatened with death, to do or act anything against honour, I would not do it; nay I would die first.   And in honour are many ingrediencies, as justice, chastity, truth, trust, gratitude, constancy, and many like.   Next, I answer that it is not out of a fantastic humour that I live so much retired, but out of self-love—not out of self-opinion.   It is just and natural for any one to love himself. Wherefore, for my pleasure and delight—my ease and peace—I live a retired life; a home life, free from the entanglements, confused clamours and rumbling noise of the world.   Here I live in a calm silence, wherein I have my contemplations free from disturbance, and my mind lives in peace and my thoughts in pleasure : they sport and play—they are not vexed with cares or worldly desires,—they are not covetous of worldly wealth or ambitious of empty titles—they are not to be caught with the baits of sensual pleasures (or rather I may say sensual follies), for they draw my senses to them, and run not out to the senses—they have no quarrelling disputes amongst them—they live friendly and sociably together—their only delight is in their own pastimes and harmless recreations—and though I do not go personally to masks, balls, and plays, yet my thoughts entertain my mind, for some of my thoughts make plays, and others act those plays on the stage of imagination, while my mind sits as a spectator. Thus my mind is entertained both with poets and players, taking as much delight as Augustus Cæsar did, to sit with his Mæcenas and hear Virgil and Horace read their works unto them. So my mind takes delight in its Mæcenas, which is Contemplation, and to have its poetical thoughts (although not like Virgil or Horace, yet such as they are) repeat their pieces: and those my mind likes best, it sends forth to the senses to write them down. None truly enjoy themselves but those who live to themselves, as I do; and it is better to be a self-lover in a retired life, than a self-seeker in a wandering humour like a vagabond. They have no constant dwelling, for, going much abroad, they dwell everywhere, and yet, to speak metaphorically, nowhere. But delights are different; for the Lady S. P. delights herself with others, and I delight myself with myself. Some delight in troubles, I delight in ease. And certainly much company cannot choose but be troublesome, for in much company are many exceptions, much envy, much suspicion, much detraction, much faction, much noise and much nonsense—and it is impossible, at least improbable for any particular person to please all the several companies they come into. Then, if particular persons be accoutered bravely they are envied, if they be attired in plain, mean garments, they are despised: if any woman be more beautiful than common, she shall be sure to have female detractors and slanderers: and if any woman be ill-favoured, it is mentioned as a reproach, although it be Nature's fault, not hers: if she be indifferently handsome, they speak of her as 'regardless:' if she be in years, they will say 'she is fitter for the grave than company:' if young, 'fitter for the school than conversation:' if of middle years, their tongues are the forerunners of her decay: if she have wealth and no titles, she is 'like meat, all fat and no blood:' and if of great title with small wealth, they say she is 'like a pudding without suet:' and if she hath both wealth and title, they hate to see her as owls hate the light: if she hath neither wealth nor title, they scorn her company. And thus the generality is to every particular. Wherefore it is impossible for any particular either to please the humours or avoid the slanders or reproaches of the generality—for every one is against all and all is against every one.

But I am not so retired as to bar myself from the company of my good friends, such as do not translate harmless and simple words to evil sense and meaning, such as are so noble as not to detract from or dispraise such persons as they take the pains to visit, or such as will not take it for neglect if I do not punctually return their visit or perhaps not visit them at any time, but will excuse or pardon my lazy humour, and not account it a disrespect. To conclude, I am more happy in my home-retirement than I believe the Lady S. P. is in her public frequentings —having a noble and kind husband, who is witty and wise company, a peaceable and quiet mind and recreative thoughts that take harmless liberty.

THEOLOGICAL DISPUTATIONS.

Madam,—You told me in your last letter that there was a great and earnest dispute between O. G. and C. O., in Divinity, to prove many things which are easier to be believed than proved. For though proof makes knowledge, yet belief doth not make proof. Though many thousands of men believe one thing or several, a thousand years, yet neither the number of men nor of years doth prove it to be true. They only prove that so many men believe it for so many years. Divinity is above all sense and reason as also all demonstration. Wherefore Faith is required in all religions, for what cannot be conceived or apprehended, must be believed. Now if the chief pillar of religion is Faith, men should believe more and dispute less, for disputations do argue weakness of Faith—nay, they make a strong Faith faint. Men spend more time in disputing than praying—rather striving to express their wit than increase their knowledge; for Divine mysteries are beyond all natural capacity.   Schoolmen have rather taught men contradictions than truth, and churchmen rather division than union.   And so, leaving O. G. and C. O. to agree if they can,

I rest, Madam, &c.

LONG PRAYERS.

MADAM,—As for the Lady P. Y., who, you say, spends most of her time in prayer, I can hardly believe God can be pleased with so many words; for why should we need to speak so many words to God, who knows our thoughts, minds and souls better than we do ourselves? Christ did not teach us long prayers, but a short one.   Nay, if it were lawful for men to similize God to his creatures (which I think it is not) God might be tired with long and tedious petitions or often repetitions.   But, Madam, good deeds are better than good words, insomuch as one good deed is better than a thousand good words; one act of upright justice or pure charity is better than a book full of prayers, a temperate life is better many times than a praying life. For we may be intemperate even in our prayers, as to be superstitious or idolatrous. In sooth every good deed is a prayer, for we do good for God's sake as being pleasing to him. A chaste, honest, just, charitable, temperate life, is a devout life; and worldly labour is devout, as to be honestly industrious to get and prudent to thrive that one may have wherewithal to give. There is no poor beggar but had rather a penny than a blessing, for they tell you that they shall 'starve with a *Dieu vous assiste,* but be relieved with a *denar.*' Wherefore the Lady P. Y. will starve herself and waste her life out before the natural time which will be a kind of self-murder: and I hold self-murder the greatest sin, though it should be done in a pious form or manner. But to help a friend in distress is better and more acceptable than to pray for a friend in distress—to relieve a beggar in distress is better than to pray for him—to attend the sick is better than to pray for the sick.[1] 'But,' you will say,

---

[1] This perhaps is too strongly stated. All the best that we can do for a friend is only temporary and limited, while in praying to God on his behalf we invoke the

'both do well.' I say, it is well said and well when it is done, but the one must not hinder the other. Wherefore we ought not to leave the world to pray, but to live in the world to act to good uses. And it is not enough to give for the poor, but to see that the poor be not cozened of their gifts. Wherefore we ought to distribute our gifts ourselves, and to be industrious to know and to find out those that do truly and not feignedly want. Neither must our gifts make the poor idle, but set the idle poor to work. But, perchance if the Lady P. Y. heard me, she would say, I was one of those that did speak more good words than act good deeds, or that I neither spent my time in praying nor pious acting. Indeed I cannot as the proud Pharisee brag and boast of my good deeds, but with the poor Publican, I must say, *Lord have mercy on me, a miserable sinner.* . . . . . But my condition

---

assistance and kindness of a friend whose power is infinite and whose gifts are of eternal value. Of the two, prayer is better, but of a certainty it ought to go hand in hand with practical benevolence, The Duchess somewhat corrects herself in the succeeding sentences.

is fitter for prayer, as having not sufficient means to do good works, my husband being robbed of all his estate, than the Lady P. Y. who hath saved all she can lay claim to. Wherefore, leaving her to her prayers of thanksgiving, and myself to prayers of petitioning,

I rest, Madam, &c.

SERVANTS.

MADAM,—I am sorry to hear you have lost so good a servant as E. L. was, for she was faithful, trusty, loving, humble, obedient, industrious, thrifty and quiet: harmlessly merry and free, yet full of respect and duty, which few servants are in this age. For most are idle, cozening, wasteful, crafty, bold, rude, murmuring, factious, treacherous and what not that is evil? But truly, Madam, the fault ought to be laid on the masters and mistresses, who either give their servants ill examples by their evil or idle life; or, through a credulous trust, which is a temptation to a poor servant—and it is part of our prayer, *Lead us not into temptation;* or

S 2

through a neglect of governing, for there is an old true saying, *The Master's eye makes the horse fat;* or, through a timorous fear of commanding, for many masters are afraid to command a peremptory servant, being more in awe of the servant, than the servant of the master; or, through much clemency, giving their servants their wills so much as that they neglect their duties; or, through their prodigality, whereby they make themselves poor to enrich their servants, so as the servant becomes greater than the master.

A good servant is a treasure, says Solomon, and so I think, to a servant, is a good master, if the servant have wit to perceive it. But a good master is to know how to command, when to command, and what to command: also when to bestow, and how much to bestow: also to fit servants to employment and employments to servants: also, how and when to restrain them and when to give them liberty: also to observe which of his servants be fit to be ruled with austerity or severity and which with clemency and to reward and punish properly, timely and justly: likewise when to make them

work and when to let them play a sport : when
to keep them at a distance and when to associate
himself with them.   And truly, I should sooner
choose to associate myself with the company
of my servants, had they good breeding, or
were capable to learn and imitate what did
belong to good behaviour, than with strangers ;
for good servants are friends as well as servants.
But, Madam, if I write any more I shall go near
to make you a servant to

Your Ladyship's Servant.

DIVERSITIES OF WIT.[*]

MADAM,—Since I wrote to you I have several
times conversed with Mrs. R. E. and I find her wit
runs in a part, like music, where there must be
several parties to play and sing several parts.
She is not a whole concert herself—neither
can she play the grounds of wit—but yet she
can make a shift to fill up a note.   And it is
to be observed that wit in several persons runs

---

[*] See ante p. 219, 'Wits.'

on several subjects, but few have general wits so as to play musically on every subject, especially without making a fault : for I have known some on some particular subjects will be wonderful witty and on others mere dunces and idiots. And for parts of wit some have gossiping wit, as *nurse wit,* also *wafer-and-hippocras wit, ale-and-cake wit*; as at christenings, churchings and other gossipings. Others have *bridal wit, gamesome wit, gaming wit, tavern wit,*—and some have *court wit.* But all these are but the scum and dregs of wit : only *scum wit* swims on the top and soon boils over, and *dreg wit* lies at the bottom and is hardly stirred without much motion to raise it up. Thus several sorts of wit run about amongst mankind. Mrs. T. E.'s wit is a *Platonic wit,* as loving friendships and the conversation of souls, but take her from the Platonics and she is gone both from wit and understanding, so, leaving her to her single self and her wit to her Platonic lover, I rest,

Madam, &c.

A GENTLEMAN'S CIVILTY TO LADIES.

MADAM,—It requires experience, skill and practice for men civilly yet courtly to entertain and
accompany women in visiting or the like. They
must sit within a respectful distance with their
hats off, and begin a discourse but let the
women follow it, which they will do until they
are out of breath. Also, they must not interrupt
them in their talk, but let them speak as
much and as long as they will, or rather *can;*.
for our will to talk is beyond our power, and
though we want not words yet we want understanding and knowledge to talk perpetually.
Neither must men contradict women though
they should talk nonsense, which oftentimes
they do, but must seem to applaud and approve
with gentle nods and bows, all they say. They
must also view their faces with admiring eyes,
though they be ill-favoured—but if they are
beautiful their eyes must be fixed on them or
seem to be dazzled. Likewise they must seem
to start at their calls and run with an affrighted

haste to obey their commands. Such and many the like ceremonies and fooleries there are of this kind from men to women, but these are rather from strangers than domestic acquaintances. And so leaving men to their constrained civilities and feigned admirations, I rest,

Madam, &c.

THE WIFE-MARKET.

MADAM,—I cannot wonder that Mrs. F. G. is so desirous of a husband, for I observe that all unmarried women, both maids and widows, are the like insomuch that there are more customers that go to Hymen's markets—which are churches, plays, balls, masks, marriages, &c.—than there are husbands to be sold. And all prices are bidden there, as beauty, birth, breeding, wit and virtue—though virtue is a coin whereof is not much. But husbands are so scarce, especially good ones, as they are at such rates that an indifferent price will not purchase them. Wherefore those that will buy them must be so rich as to be able to bestow an extraordinary price of beauty, birth, breeding, wit or virtue—and yet there's much ado to purchase one—nay some cannot be had without all these joined into one. Venus's markets are so well stored of all sorts and degrees of titles, professions, ages and the like, as that they are as cheap as old mackerel; and all coins are current there but virtue, whereof none is ever offered. 'Tis true the markets of Venus and Hymen are in one and the same city or place, but Hymen and Venus sell apart. . . . . . . I rest,

Madam, &c.

A PURITAN DAME.

MADAM,—Yesterday Mrs. P. I. was here to visit me, who prayed me to present her humble service to you; but since you saw her she has become an altered woman, as being a sanctified soul, a spiritual sister. She hath left curling her hair, black patches are become abominable to her, laced shoes and galoshoes are steps to pride, to go bare-necked she accounts worse than adultery: fans, ribbons, pendants, necklaces and the like are the temptations of Satan and the signs of damnation. But she is not only transformed in her dress, but her garb and speech and all her discourse, insomuch as you would not know her if you saw her, unless you were informed who she was. She speaks of nothing but heaven and purification, and after some discourse she asked me 'What posture I thought was the best to be used in prayer?' I said 'I thought no posture was more becoming, nor did fit devotion better, than kneeling, for that posture did in a manner acknowledge from whence we came and to what we shall return: for the scripture says *From earth we came and to earth we shall return.*' Then she spoke of prayers and is all for extemporary prayers: I told her that 'the more words we used in prayer the worse they were accepted, for I thought a silent adoration was better accepted of God than a self-conceited babbling.' Then she asked me 'If I thought one might not be refined by tempering his passions and appetites, or by banishing the worst of them from the soul and body to that degree as to be a deity or so divine as to be above the nature of man?' I said, 'No, for put the case that men could turn brass or iron, or such gross metals into gold and refine that gold unto its height of purity yet it would be but a metal still; so the most refined man would be but human still. Nay take the best of godly men, such as have been refined by grace, prayer and fasting to the degree of saints, yet they were but men still, so long as the body and soul were joined together: but when these were separated, what the soul would be, whether a god, a devil, a spirit or nothing, I could not tell.' With that she lifted up her eyes and departed from me, believing I was one of the wicked and reprobate, not capable of saving grace, so as I believe she will not come near me again lest her purity should be defiled in my company. The next thing we shall hear of her will be that she has become ·a preaching sister. But leaving her to her self-relying, I return to acknowledge myself,

Madam, &c.

MODE.

MADAM,—I have observed that there are amongst mankind as often mode-phrases in speech as mode-fashions in clothes and behaviour: and so moded are they that their discourse is as much decked with those phrases, as their clothes with several-coloured ribbons, or hats with feathers, or bodies with affected motions. And whosoever doth discourse out of the mode is as much despised as if their clothes or behaviours were out of fashion. They are accounted fools or ill-bred persons. Indeed most men and women in this age, in most nations in Europe, are nothing but mode; as mode-minds, mode-bodies, mode-appetites, mode-behaviours, mode-clothes, mode-pastimes or vices, mode-speeches and conversations. And what is strange they have minds according to the mode, as to have a mode-judgment. For all will give their judgments and opinions according to the mode, and they love and hate according to the mode, they are courageous or cowardly according to the mode, approve or dislike according to the mode, nay their wits are pointed according to the mode, as to raillery, buffoonly jest and the like—for better wit is not usually the mode, as being always out of fashion amongst your mode-gallants: but true and good wit lives with the serious of all time. Grave, experienced and wise men give their judgment not according to the mode or fashion but according to probability, sense and reason. Neither do they say 'Such or such a thing will or shall be or is so, Why? Because it is the general opinion:' but they say 'Such or such a thing may be or is likely to be, or is so, Why? Because there is a probability or reason of it.' Neither do the just or wise hate or love, approve or dislike, because it is the mode—as to hate what is not generally loved or love what is not generally hated, or despise what is generally disliked or admire what is generally commended, but they hate what is really bad, wicked or base, and not what is thought so: and love what is really good, virtuous and worthy, not for the general opinion but for the truth. And they admire and commend, despise or scorn, dislike or disapprove that which is despicable or discommendable or scornable . . . . They speak not with mode phrases but such words as are most plain to be understood, and their behaviours are those which are most manly and least apish, fantastical or constrained. Their clothes are such as are most useful, easy and becoming. Their appetites do not relish mode-meats or sauces because they have the mode *haut goût*, but relish best what is most pleasing and savoury to their taste. Neither do they affect mode-songs or sounds because they are in the fashion to be sung or played, but because they are well-set tunes or well composed music or witty songs or well sung by good voices or well played on good instruments. They do not follow mode-vices or vanities for fashion . . . . nor the exercises that are in mode—but those they like best. If it be the mode to play at tennis, or paille-maille[1]

---

[1] 'A game, of which the most common memorial remains in the street once appropriated to that use, as was afterwards the *Mall* in St. James's Park. It is

or the like—if he like better to ride or fence, he will let alone the mode exercises and use his own. If it be the mode pastime to play at cards or dice and he like better to write or read he will leave the mode pastime and follow his own. If it be the mode custom to dine and sup and meet at ordinaries and taverns and he like better to sup and dine at home alone he will not go to ordinaries or taverns. Neither will he ride post because it is the mode but because his affairs require it. But leaving the modists to their mode clothes, oaths, phrases, courtships, behaviours, garbs and motions, to their mode meats, drinks, pastimes, exercises, pleasures, vanities and vices, to their mode songs, tunes, dances, fiddles and voices, to their mode judgments, opinions and

---

derived from *pale maille*, French: at which word Cotgrave thus describes the game: " A game, wherein a round box bowle, is with a mallet struck through a high arch of iron (standing, at either end of an ally, one,) which he that can do at the fewest blows, or at the number agreed on, wins." Properly, I believe, the place for playing was called the *mall*, the stick employed *palemail*.'—Nares Glossary.

wits, to their mode quarrels and friendships, to their mode lying and dissembling: I rest,

Madam, &c.

SPEAKING THE BEST OF ALL MEN.

MADAM,—I was reading to-day several satires of several famous poets, wherein I find that they praise themselves and dispraise all others, which expresses a great self-dotage and a very ill-nature. Madam, I wish all writers would use their pens as your noble Lord and Husband orders his discourse in speech, to speak the best of all men, and to bury their faults in silence, which would make virtue an emulation and faults such a novelty as men would be ashamed to commit them. I am,

Madam, &c.

A CONVENTICLE.

MADAM,—Since I last wrote to you,[1] I have been to hear Mrs. P. I. preach, for now she is,

---

[1] See page 265, 'A Puritan Dame.'

as I believed she would be, a preaching sister.
There were a great many holy sisters and holy
brethren met together, where many took their
turns to preach: for as they are for liberty
of conscience, so they are for liberty of
preaching. But there were more sermons than
learning and more words than reason. Mrs.
P. I. began, but her sermon I do not well
remember, and after she had sighed and winded
out her devotion, a holy brother stood up
and preached thus, as I shall briefly relate
to you:

*Dearly beloved brethren and sisters,—We are
gathered together in the Lord with purity of
spirit to preach his Word amongst us. We are
the chosen and the elect children of the Lord,
who have glorified spirits and sanctified souls.
We have the spirit of God in us which inspires
us to pray and to preach as also to call upon
his name and to remember him of his promise
to unite and gather us together unto his New
Jerusalem, separating us from reprobates, that
we may not be defiled with their presence; for
you dear brethren know by the spirit that they*

are not the children of the Lord but Satan's children—they are the children of darkness we the children of light ; we are glorified and sanctified by supernatural grace, we are a peculiar people and the holy prophets of the Lord, to foresee foretell and declare his will and pleasure ; also we are to encourage and comfort the Saints in affliction and consolation and to help them to present their Sanctified sighs, tears and groans unto the Lord : but the spirit moveth me to pray and to leave off preaching wherefore let us pray.

So after the holy brother had done his prayer Mr. M. N., who was there, pulled off his peruke and put on a night-cap, wherein he appeared so like a holy brother as they took him for one of their sect, and he preached this following sermon :

Dearly beloved brethren,—We are here met in a congregation together, some to teach, others to learn : but neither the teaching nor learning can be any other way but natural and according to human capacity, for we cannot be celestial whilst we are terrestrial, neither can we be glorified whilst we are mortal, nor yet can we arrive to the purity of saints or angels, whilst we are subject to natural imperfections both in body and mind : But there are some men that believe they are or at least may be so pure in spirit by saving grace as to be sanctified, and to be so much filled with the Holy Ghost as to have spiritual visions, and ordinarily to have conversation with God believing God to be a common companion to their idle imaginations. But this opinion proceeds from an extraordinary self-love, self-pride and self-ambition, as to believe they are the only fit companions for God himself and that not any of God's Creatures are or were worthy to be favoured but they, much less to be made God's privy council as they believe they are—as to know his will and pleasure, his decrees and destinies, which indeed are not to be known, for the Creator is too mighty for a Creature to comprehend him. Wherefore let us humbly pray to what we cannot conceive.

But before he had quite ended his sermon the holy flock began to bustle, and at last went quite out of the room so that he might have prayed by himself had not I and one

or two ladies more that were of my company
stayed, and when he had done his short prayer
he told me and the other ladies, that he had
done that which the great council of state could
not do, for he had by one short discourse
dispersed a company of sectaries without noise
or disturbance.   I subscribe myself,

Madam, &c.

SCRIPTURE OUGHT NOT TO BE PARA-PHRASED.

Madam,—You were pleased to tell me in your
last letter, that you had spent most of the morning in reading a new work, which is highly commended, *viz.*, Paraphrases on the life of some
of the holy prophets and kings.   I cannot say,
but it may be pleasing to read but I doubt
whether it will be well to write it; for whosoever
doth heighten the sacred scriptures by poetical
expressions doth translate it to the nature of
a romance, for the ground of a romance is
for the most part truth, but upon those truths
are feignings built; and certainly the scripture,

and feignings ought not to be mixed together. For so holy a truth ought not to be expressed fabulously. Wherefore in my opinion no subject is so unfit for poetical fancies as the scripture; for though poetry is divine yet it ought not to obstruct and obscure the truth of sacred historical prose. 'Tis true Divine poetical raptures such as *David's* psalms are commendable and admirable, being an effect of a devout soul and zealous spirit, which flames into poetical raptures and is inspired with a divine influence delivering itself through harmonious numbers, sympathetical rhythms, elegant phrases and eloquent language, all which is presented to God from the heart as an offering or sacrifice of thanksgiving, or an imploring of mercy, or an humble acknowledgment of sins and promise of amendment, which sacred poems are expressed in a tragic vein concerning sins, and in a comic vein concerning blessings. And poets in their morning hymns are like the larks that begin the day, and in their evening hymns like the nightingales which begin the night. Thus divine poets are heaven's birds, that sing to God, and their divine poems are their brood which are kept in the cage of memory, and sing their parents' notes to after ages. But, Madam, perchance you will think I am peremptory, to give my opinion of the poet's work before I see it, but I give my opinion only upon the ground of his work, which is the scripture, saying it ought not to be paraphrased. Besides, I give it from my conscience not from my conceited brain, and perchance I may alter my opinion upon more rational arguments from those that are more learned and knowing than myself; and if your opinion differs from mine pray send it me in your next letter, for I would willingly be of your opinion believing you cannot err, nor can I, in expressing myself,

Madam,

Your very faithful friend and devoted servant.

GOSSIPING.

MADAM,—In your last letter you say that the lady G. P. carried a letter she received from Mrs. O. B.

from company to company, to jest at, because it was not indited after the courtly phrase, but after the old manner and way, beginning thus : *After my hearty commendation hoping you are in good health, as I am at the writing hereof; this is to let you understand, &c.* But I know not why anybody should jest at it, for 'tis friendly to send commendations and to wish our friends good health. And certainly friendly and kind expressions are to be preferred before courtly compliments; the first sounds like real truth, the other may be demonstrated to be feigning, for all compliments exceed the truth. 'Tis true the style of letters alters and changes as the fashion of clothes doth, but fashions are not always changed for more commodious or becoming ones, but for the sake of variety, for an old fashion may be more useful and graceful than a modern fashion. But I believe the lady G. P. carried Mrs. O. B.'s letter about with her, for a pretence to visit company, like as gossips do cakes and other junkets to their neighbours, the junkets increasing the company and the company the junkets; so the lady G. P. out of a luxury to talking and company, like as other gossips out of a luxury to talking and eating, carried the letter to show her several acquaintance sport, or to get other acquaintance. And if she had not had that letter 'tis likely she would have found some other pretence rather than have stayed at home. Indeed, one may say that in this age there is a malignant contagion of gossiping, for not only one woman infects another, but the women infect the men, and then one man infects another; nay, it spreads so much as it takes hold even on young children, so strong and infectious is this malignity. But if any will avoid it they must every morning anoint the soles of their feet with the oil of slackness and bathe every limb in a bath of rest, then they must put into their ears some drops of quiet to strengthen the brain against vaporous noise and stop their ears with a little wool of deafness to keep out the wind of idle discourse, also they must wash their eyes with the water of obscurity lest the glaring light of vanity should weaken them, and they must take some electuary of contemplation, which is very soverain to comfort the spirits, and they must drink cooling juleps of discretion which are good against the fever of company, and if they take some jelly of restraint they will find it to be an excellent remedy against this malignity, only they must take great care lest they be too relax to persuasion, but rather so restringent as to be obstinate from entering into a concourse; for there is nothing more dangerous in all malignant diseases than throngs or crowds of people; and this is the best preparative against the plague of gossiping. But for fear with writing too long a letter I should fall into that disease I take my leave and rest,

Madam,

Your very faithful friend and servant.

CONVERSATION REQUIRES WITTY OPPOSITES.

MADAM,—Here was the Lord W. N. to visit me whose discourse, as you say, is like as a pair of bellows to a spark of fire in a chimney, where are coals or wood; for as this spark would sooner go out than enkindle the fuel, if it were not blown, so his discourse doth set the hearers brain on a light flame, which heats the wit, and enlightens the understanding. The truth is, great wits might be thought, or seem fools, if they had not wit to discourse, but the greatest wits that are, or ever were, cannot discourse wittily, unless they either imagine or else have a real witty opposite to discourse wittily too. Like as those that can skilfully fence, cannot fence unless they have an opposite to fence with; or like as those that can skilfully play at tennis, cannot play, unless they have a skilful opposite; they may toss the ball, but not play a game; the same it is in conversation and discourse; there is none can discourse well, wisely or wittily, but with wise and witty opposites, otherwise their discourse will be extravagant, and as it were out of time or season. But the Lord W. N.'s wit is a well seasoned wit, both for reason, time and company, to which I leave him and rest,

Madam,

Your faithful friend and servant.

TRUTH AND FLATTERY.

MADAM,—In your last letter you desired me to write some letters of compliment, as also some panegyricks; but I must intreat you to excuse me, for my style in writing is too plain and simple for such courtly works; besides give me leave to inform you that I am a servant to Truth and not to Flattery; although I confess I rather lose than gain in my mistress's service. For she is poor and naked, and hath not those means to advance her servants as Flattery hath who gives plenty of words and is prodigal of praise and is clothed in a flourishing style, imbroidered with oratory. But my mistress Truth hath no need of such adornings neither doth she give many words, and seldom any praise, so as her servants have not any thing to live on òr by but mere honesty which rather starveth than feeds any creature. Yet howsoever I being bred in her service from my youth will never quit her till death takes me away; and if

I can serve you by serving her, command
me and I shall honestly obey you and so
rest,

Madam,
your faithful Friend and Servant.

THE END.

INDEX.

OXFORD:

By T. Combe, M.A., E. B. Gardner, E. Pickard Hall, and J. H. Stacy,

PRINTERS TO THE UNIVERSITY.

MACMILLAN'S

GOLDEN TREASURY SERIES.

UNIFORMLY printed in 18mo., with Vignette Titles by Sir
NOEL PATON, T. WOOLNER, W. HOLMAN HUNT, J. E.
MILLAIS, ARTHUR HUGHES, &c. Engraved on Steel by
JEENS. Bound in extra cloth, 4s. 6d. each volume. Also
kept in morocco and calf bindings.

> *"Messrs. Macmillan have, in their Golden Treasury Series, especially
> provided editions of standard works, volumes of selected poetry, and
> original compositions, which entitle this series to be called classical.
> Nothing can be better than the literary execution, nothing more
> elegant than the material workmanship."*—BRITISH QUARTERLY
> REVIEW.

The Golden Treasury of the Best Songs and
LYRICAL POEMS IN THE ENGLISH LANGUAGE.
Selected and arranged, with Notes, by FRANCIS TURNER
PALGRAVE.

> *"This delightful little volume, the Golden Treasury, which contains
> many of the best original lyrical pieces and songs in our language,
> grouped with care and skill, so as to illustrate each other like the
> pictures in a well-arranged gallery."*—QUARTERLY REVIEW.

The Children's Garland from the best Poets.
Selected and arranged by COVENTRY PATMORE.

> *"It includes specimens of all the great masters in the art of poetry,
> selected with the matured judgment of a man concentrated on
> obtaining insight into the feelings and tastes of childhood, and*

D

desirous to awaken its finest impulses, to cultivate its keenest s[en]bilities."—MORNING POST. .

The Book of Praise. From the Best English Hymn Wri[ters]. Selected and arranged by Sir ROUNDELL PALMER. *A New* *Enlarged Edition.*

> *" All previous compilations of this kind must undeniably for* *present give place to the Book of Praise. . . . The selection* *been made throughout with sound judgment and critical taste.* *pains involved in this compilation must have been immense,* *bracing, as it does, every writer of note in this special provin[ce]* *English literature, and ranging over the most widely diver[se]* *tracks of religious thought."*—SATURDAY REVIEW.

The Fairy Book; the Best Popular Fairy Stories. Selected rendered anew by the Author of "JOHN HALIFAX, GENTLEMA[N]."

> *" A delightful selection, in a delightful external form ; full of* *physical splendour and vast opulence of proper fairy tales.*[—] SPECTATOR.

The Ballad Book. A Selection of the Choicest British Ball[ads]. Edited by WILLIAM ALLINGHAM.

> *" His taste as a judge of old poetry will be found, by all acquainted [with]* *the various readings of old English ballads, true enough to ju[stify]* *his undertaking so critical a task."*—SATURDAY REVIEW.

The Jest Book. The Choicest Anecdotes and Sayings. Selec[ted] and arranged by MARK LEMON.

> *" The fullest and best jest book that has yet appeared."*—SATUR[DAY] REVIEW. .

Bacon's Essays and Colours of Good and Ev[il]. With Notes and Glossarial Index. By W. ALDIS WRIGHT, M[.A.]

> *" The beautiful little edition of Bacon's Essays, now before us, [is a]* *credit to the taste and scholarship of Mr. Aldis Wright. . . .* *puts the reader in possession of all the essential literary facts [and]* *chronology necessary for reading the Essays in connection w[ith]* *Bacon's life and times."*—SPECTATOR. *" By far the most comp[lete]* *as well as the most elegant edition we possess."*—WESTMINST[ER] REVIEW.

'he **Pilgrim's Progress** from this World to that which is to come.   By JOHN BUNYAN.

"*A beautiful and scholarly reprint.*"—SPECTATOR.

'he **Sunday Book of Poetry for the Young.** Selected and arranged by C. F. ALEXANDER.

"*A well-selected volume of Sacred Poetry.*"—SPECTATOR.

Book of Golden Deeds of All Times and All Countries. Gathered and narrated anew.   By the Author of "THE HEIR OF REDCLYFFE."

"*. . . To the young, for whom it is especially intended, as a most interesting collection of thrilling tales well told; and to their elders, as a useful handbook of reference, and a pleasant one to take up when their wish is to while away a weary half-hour.   We have seen no prettier gift-book for a long time.*"—ATHENÆUM.

ie **Poetical Works of Robert Burns.** Edited, with Biographical Memoir, Notes, and Glossary, by ALEXANDER SMITH.   Two Vols.

"*Beyond all question this is the most beautiful edition of Burns yet out.*"—EDINBURGH DAILY REVIEW.

.e **Adventures of Robinson Crusoe.** Edited from the Original Edition by J. W. CLARK, M.A., Fellow of Trinity College, Cambridge.

"*Mutilated and modified editions of this English classic are so much the rule, that a cheap and pretty copy of it, rigidly exact to the original, will be a prize to many book-buyers.*"—EXAMINER.

e **Republic of Plato.** TRANSLATED into ENGLISH, with Notes by J. Ll. DAVIES, M.A. and D. J. VAUGHAN, M.A.

"*A dainty and cheap little edition.*"—EXAMINER.

e **Song Book.** Words and Tunes from the best Poets and Musicians.   Selected and arranged by JOHN HULLAH. Professor of Vocal Music in King's College, London.

MACMILLAN'S

GLOBE LIBRARY.

Beautifully printed on toned paper and bound in cloth extra, gilt edges, price 4s. 6d. each ; in cloth plain, 3s. 6d.   Also kept in a variety of calf and morocco bindings at moderate prices.

Books, Wordsworth says, are

> "the spirit breathed
> By dead men to their kind ;"

and the aim of the publishers of the Globe Library has been to make it possible for the universal kin of English-speaking men to hold communion with the loftiest "spirits of the mighty dead ;" to put within the reach of all classes *complete* and *accurate* editions, carefully and clearly printed upon the best paper, in a convenient form, at a moderate price, of the works of the MASTER-MINDS OF ENGLISH LITERATURE, and occasionally of foreign literature in an attractive English dress.

The Editors, by their scholarship and special study of their authors, are competent to afford every assistance to readers of all kinds : this assistance is rendered by original biographies, glossaries of unusual or obsolete words, and critical and explanatory notes.

The publishers hope, therefore, that these Globe Edition may prove worthy of acceptance by all classes wherever th English Language is spoken, and by their universal circul. tion justify their distinctive epithet ; while at the same tim they spread and nourish a common sympathy with nature most "finely touched" spirits, and thus help a little t "make the whole world kin."

> *The* SATURDAY REVIEW *says : " The Globe Editions are admirab for their scholarly editing, their typographical excellence, their com pendious form, and their cheapness." The* BRITISH QUARTERL REVIEW *says : " In compendiousness, elegance, and scholarlines the Globe Editions of Messrs. Macmillan surpass any popular seri of our classics hitherto given to the public. As near an approac to miniature perfection as has ever been made."*

Shakespeare's Complete Works. Edited by W. G CLARK, M.A., and W. ALDIS WRIGHT, M. A., of Trinity College Cambridge, Editors of the "Cambridge Shakespeare. Witl Glossary. pp. 1,075. Price 3*s*. 6*d*.

> *This edition aims at presenting a perfectly reliable text of the complet works of " the foremost man in all literature." The text is essen tially the same as that of the "Cambridge Shakespeare." Appende is a Glossary containing the meaning of every word in the text whicl is either obsolete or is used in an antiquated or unusual sense This, combined with the method used to indicate corrupted readings serves to a great extent the purpose of notes. The* ATHENÆUM *say. this edition is " a marvel of beauty, cheapness, and compactness. . . . For the busy man, above all for the working student, this i the best of all existing Shakespeares." And the* PALL MALL GAZETTE *observes : " To have produced the {complete works o the world's greatest poet in such a form, and at a price within the reach of every one, is of itself almost sufficient to give the publishers a claim to be considered public benefactors."*

Spenser's Complete Works. Edited from the Original Editions and Manuscripts, by R. MORRIS, with a Memoir by J. W. HALES, M.A. With Glossary. pp. lv., 736. Price 3*s*. 6*d*.

*genuine pathos, pure passionate love. The exhaustive glossar index and the copious notes will make all the purely Scotch poe intelligible even to an Englishman. Burns's letters must be r by all who desire fully to appreciate the poet's character, to se on all its many sides. Explanatory notes are prefixed to m of these letters, and Burns's Journals kept during his Bor and Highland Tours, are appended. Following the prefi biography by the editor, is a Chronological Table of Burns's L and Works. "Admirable in all respects."—*SPECTATOR. *" 1 cheapest, the most perfect, and the most interesting edition which I ever been published."—*BELL'S MESSENGER.

Robinson Crusoe. Edited after the Original Editions, witl

Biographical Introduction by HENRY KINGSLEY. pp. xxxi., 6(
Price 3*s.* 6*d.*

Of this matchless truth-like story, it is scarcely possible to find unabridged edition. This edition may be relied upon as contain the whole of "Robinson Crusoe" as it came from the pen of author, without mutilation, and with all peculiarities religiou preserved. These points, combined with its handsome paper, la clear type, and moderate price, ought to render this par exceller *the "Globe," the Universal edition of Defoe's fascinating narrati "A most excellent and in every way desirable edition."—*COU CIRCULAR. *"Macmillan's ' Globe' Robinson Crusoe is a book have and to keep."—*MORNING STAR.

Goldsmith's Miscellaneous Works. Edited, w

Biographical Introduction, by Professor MASSON. pp. lx., 6(
Globe 8vo. 3*s.* 6*d.*

*This volume comprehends the whole of the prose and poetical wo of this most genial of English authors, those only being exclu which are mere compilations. They are all accurately reprin from the most reliable editions. The faithfulness, fulness, and li rary merit of the biography are sufficiently attested by the name its author, Professor Masson. It contains many interesting an dotes which will give the reader an insight into Goldsmil character, and many graphic pictures of the literary life of Lon during the middle of last century. "Such an admirable comp dium of the facts of Goldsmith's life, and so careful and minute delineation of the mixed traits of his peculiar character as to a very model of a literary biography in little."—*SCOTSMAN.

Pope's Poetical Works. Edited, with Notes and Introductory Memoir, by ADOLPHUS WILLIAM WARD, M.A., Fellow of St. Peter's College, Cambridge, and Professor of History in Owens College, Manchester. pp. lii., 508. Globe 8vo. 3s. 6d.

This edition contains all Pope's poems, translations, and adaptations, —his now superseded Homeric translations alone being omitted. The text, carefully revised, is taken from the best editions; Pope's own use of capital letters and apostrophised syllables, frequently necessary to an understanding of his meaning, has been preserved; while his uncertain spelling and his frequently perplexing interpunctuation have been judiciously amended. Abundant notes are added, including Pope's own, the best of those of previous editors, and many which are the result of the study and research of the present editor. The introductory Memoir will be found to shed considerable light on the political, social, and literary life of the period in which Pope filled so large a space. The LITERARY CHURCHMAN *remarks:* "*The editor's own notes and introductory memoir are excellent, the memoir alone would be cheap and well worth buying at the price of the whole volume.*"

Dryden's Poetical Works. Edited, with a Memoir, Revised Text, and Notes, by W. D. CHRISTIE, M.A., of Trinity College, Cambridge. pp. lxxxvii., 662. Globe 8vo. 3s. 6d.

A study of Dryden's works is absolutely necessary to anyone who wishes to understand thoroughly, not only the literature, but also the political and religious history of the eventful period when he lived and reigned as literary dictator. In this edition of his works, which comprises several specimens of his vigorous prose, the text has been thoroughly corrected and purified from many misprints and small changes often materially affecting the sense, which had been allowed to slip in by previous editors. The old spelling has been retained where it is not altogether strange or repulsive. Besides an exhaustive Glossary, there are copious Notes, critical, historical, biographical, and explanatory; and the biography contains the results of considerable original research, which has served to shed light on several hitherto obscure circumstances connected with the life and parentage of the poet. "*An admirable edition, the result of great research and of a careful revision of the text. The memoir prefixed contains, within less than ninety pages, as much sound criticism and as comprehensive a biography as the student of Dryden need desire.*"—PALL MALL GAZETTE.

Cowper's Poetical Works.   Edited, with Notes a[nd]
Biographical Introduction, by WILLIAM BENHAM, Vicar [of]
Addington and Professor of Modern History in Queen's Colleg[e]
London.   pp. lxxiii., 536.   Globe 8vo.   3s. 6d.

> *This volume contains, arranged under seven heads, the whole [of]*
> *Cowper's own poems, including several never before published, a[nd]*
> *all his translations except that of Homer's "Iliad."   The text [is]*
> *taken from the original editions, and Cowper's own notes are giv[en]*
> *at the foot of the page, while many explanatory notes by the edit[or]*
> *himself are appended to the volume.   In the very full Memoir [it]*
> *will be found, that much new light has been thrown on some [of]*
> *the most difficult passages of Cowper's spiritually chequered li[fe]*
> *"Mr. Benham's edition of Cowper is one of permanent valu[e]*
> *The biographical introduction is excellent, full of informatio[n]*
> *singularly neat and readable and modest—indeed too modest [in]*
> *its comments.   The notes are concise and accurate, and the edit[or]*
> *has been able to discover and introduce some hitherto unprint[ed]*
> *matter.   Altogether the book is a very excellent one."—*SATURDA[Y]
> REVIEW.

Morte d'Arthur.—SIR THOMAS MALORY'S BOOK O[F]
KING ARTHUR AND OF HIS NOBLE KNIGHTS O[F]
THE ROUND TABLE.   The original Edition of CAXTO[N]
revised for Modern Use.   With an Introduction by Sir EDWAR[D]
STRACHEY, Bart.   pp. xxxvii., 509.   Globe 8vo.   3s. 6d.

> *This volume contains the cream of the legends of chivalry whic[h]*
> *have gathered round the shadowy King Arthur and his Knigh[ts]*
> *of the Round Table.   Tennyson has drawn largely on them in h[is]*
> *cycle of Arthurian Idylls.   The language is simple and quaint [as]*
> *that of the Bible, and the many stories of knightly adventure [of]*
> *which the book is made up, are fascinating as those of the "Arabia[n]*
> *Nights."   The great moral of the book is to " do after the good, an[d]*
> *leave the evil."   There was a want of an edition of the work at [a]*
> *moderate price, suitable for ordinary readers, and especially fo[r]*
> *boys: such an edition the present professes to be.   The Introductio[n]*
> *contains an account of the Origin and Matter of the book, the Tex[t]*
> *and its several Editions, and an Essay on Chivalry, tracing it[s]*
> *history from its origin to its decay.   Notes are appended, and [a]*

Glossary of such words as require explanation. "It is with perfect confidence that we recommend this edition of the old romance to every class of readers."—PALL MALL GAZETTE.

The Works of Virgil. Rendered into English Prose, with Introductions, Notes, Running Analysis, and an Index. By JAMES LONSDALE, M.A., late Fellow and Tutor of Balliol College, Oxford, and Classical Professor in King's College, London; and SAMUEL LEE, M.A., Latin Lecturer at University College, London. pp. 288. Price 3*s.* 6*d.*

The publishers believe that an accurate and readable translation of all the works of Virgil is perfectly in accordance with the object of the "Globe Library." A new prose-translation has therefore been made by two competent scholars, who have rendered the original faithfully into simple Bible-English, without paraphrase; and at the same time endeavoured to maintain as far as possible the rhythm and majestic flow of the original. On this latter point the DAILY TELEGRAPH *says, "The endeavour to preserve in some degree a rhythm in the prose rendering is almost invariably successful and pleasing in its effect;" and the* EDUCATIONAL TIMES, *that it "may be readily recommended as a model for young students for rendering the poet into English." The General Introduction will be found full of interesting information as to the life of Virgil, the history of opinion concerning his writings, the notions entertained of him during the Middle Ages, editions of his works, his influence on modern poets and on education. To each of his works is prefixed a critical and explanatory introduction, and important aid is afforded to the thorough comprehension of each production by the running Analysis. Appended is an Index of all the proper names and the most important subjects occurring throughout the poems and introductions. "A more complete edition of Virgil in English it is scarcely possible to conceive than the scholarly work before us."* —GLOBE.

R. CLAY, SONS, AND TAYLOR, PRINTERS, BREAD STREET HILL.